She tensed and bit her lip.

"So," he said, barely audibly. "Things *have* changed. You'd better tell me, Clare. Is there a new man in your life? Has someone swept you off your feet—and taken over where I left off?"

A mixture of shock and outrage poured through her. "No," she said intensely. What do you think I am?"

"Changed," Lachlan said deliberately. "You always were beautiful to my eyes, but now you're like a rose that's opening in all its glory. And you're taking weekends off, lying on the beach—something's happened to you, Clare. Is it true love? It surely has to be something cataclysmic, because nothing I ever did produced this."

"In a way you did, Lachlan. I...you see... I'm pregnant."

EXPECTING

She's sexy,
successful...
and
PREGNANT!

Relax and enjoy our fabulous series about
spirited women and gorgeous men, whose
passion results in pregnancies...sometimes
unexpected! Of course, the birth of a baby is
always a joyful event, and we can guarantee that
our characters will become besotted moms and
dads—but what happened in those nine
months before?

Share the surprises, emotions, dramas and
suspense as our parents-to-be come to terms
with the prospect of bringing a new little life into
the world.... All will discover that the business of
making babies brings with it the most special
love of all....

Look out next month for:
The Boss's Baby (#2064)
by Miranda Lee

LINDSAY ARMSTRONG

Having His Babies

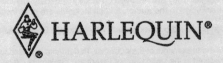

TORONTO • NEW YORK • LONDON
AMSTERDAM • PARIS • SYDNEY • HAMBURG
STOCKHOLM • ATHENS • TOKYO • MILAN • MADRID
PRAGUE • WARSAW • BUDAPEST • AUCKLAND

ISBN 0-373-12057-5

HAVING HIS BABIES

First North American Publication 1999.

Copyright © 1999 by Lindsay Armstrong.

CHAPTER ONE

'I BEG your pardon?'

'Well, we could do a blood test but I don't think it's necessary—from what you've told me and from this sample there seems to be no doubt. Congratulations, Clare!'

Clare Montrose stared at her doctor, a woman in her late thirties whose bright, cheerful expression faded somewhat as she took in her patient's stunned eyes.

'You...didn't expect or plan this?' Valerie Martin queried.

'No. That is to say, no.' Clare swallowed. 'Are you sure? I'm on the pill, as you know, and I've never forgotten to take it.'

'Ah. Yes, I did prescribe a low dose, so-called mini-pill but I also explained the circumstances that can sometimes interfere with its effectiveness if you remember, Clare.'

Clare opened her mouth, closed it and said shakily, 'But...but nothing like that, well, not really— Oh, no,' she said hollowly. 'I didn't even stop to think!'

'Tell me,' Valerie said gently.

'I had a twenty-four-hour virus a while back,' Clare said helplessly. 'Nausea, gastric upset, but two days later I was as right as rain and I didn't give it a second thought. I was run off my feet at the time, too so—you mean *that* could have done it?'

'It could. It's not common but it could if it was a severe enough bout. Have you had no other symptoms? This—' Valerie smiled a little ruefully '—seems to have come like a bolt from the blue.'

'No. Well, I came to see you because my cycle seemed to have gone haywire but I've had that problem before—before I went on the pill, anyway,' she amended, and sat back dazedly. 'How much pregnant?'

'We need to discuss a few dates but I would estimate six to eight weeks.'

Clare pulled her diary from her purse and did some rapid mental arithmetic. 'Yes,' she said hollowly at last, 'I imagine that would be about right—eight weeks. But why haven't I had any morning sickness or—anything?'

'We don't all get it and we don't all get it at the same time; you may be one of the lucky ones but I'd be surprised if you didn't very shortly see some changes. Like a loss of appetite or suddenly being starving all the time. Such as feeling sleepy a lot of the time...'

'Craving jam on pickles, that kind of thing,' Clare said gloomily. 'How could this happen to me?'

'Clare.' Valerie Martin stopped and watched her intently for a moment. And marvelled inwardly because she knew Clare Montrose quite well. They had their practices in the same building in the seaside town of Lennox Head although Clare practised law. And over the past few years this tall, quietly spoken though assured and obviously very intelligent girl had expanded the sleepy practice she'd bought to keep pace with the town's growth and turned it into a profitable one with a growing reputation that was spreading throughout the district.

And yet, Valerie mused, over the matter of getting herself pregnant, there seems to be a certain naiveté. Not quite what I would have expected from someone who can be as coolly competent as she undoubtedly can.

'Clare...I don't like to pry, but...is it not Lachlan?'

Clare blinked her eyes that were the colour of the sea at certain times, a greeny blue that could best be described as aquamarine, and her face, beneath shining dark hair parted on the side and falling in a curly bob, reddened.

Valerie looked fleetingly amused. 'You can't keep anything a secret in this village, my dear, but particularly not Lachlan Hewitt. His family has been in the area for generations; they've been shire councillors and the biggest landowners around Alstonville, Ballina and Lennox Head ever since I can remember. Besides, I didn't think you were trying to keep it a secret.'

'We weren't,' Clare said, gloomily again. 'That is to say, once his divorce came through, it didn't seem to be anyone's business but our own, but...we weren't exactly trying to flaunt it.'

'I'm sure you weren't. These things get noticed, though. Lachlan is the kind of man who gets noticed—as you're the kind of woman who does, my dear. So...this wasn't on the agenda?'

'No,' Clare said baldly after a moment.

'Circumstances change cases, as I'm sure I don't have to point out to a lawyer, but...' Dr Martin paused '…I'm also sure I don't have to point out to you that there are other—options.'

Clare breathed raggedly and her eyes widened. 'Oh. No, that's not an option—the thought of it just—' She shivered then shrugged. 'I don't think I could do it.'

'Well, I'm glad to hear you say so but that's only a personal preference of mine. However, you're—' she glanced down at the card in front of her '—twenty-seven, which is by no means too old to be having a baby. But we don't get any younger and, while it may not have been on your *conscious* agenda, perhaps you should take into account that it may have been on your unconscious one…'

When Clare was back in her office, she grimaced because the thought of her biological clock ticking away unbeknownst to her was disturbing.

She looked around, at her framed degree on the wall, at the cool eggshell-blue walls and sapphire carpet, the vast mahogany desk she was inordinately proud of—an antique she'd unearthed and had restored—at the silver-framed paintings on the wall, and she sat down with a deep sigh.

She'd instructed her receptionist to hold all calls for half an hour and knew they'd be piling up like a tidal wave. Business was booming, and although she had an articled clerk and a legal secretary, what she really needed was a qualified solicitor to take some of the pressure off her—more than ever now, she mused, and gazed at one particular picture on the wall.

It wasn't a painting but an aerial photo of a suburban housing estate across the Pacific Highway from Lennox Head, and it was where so much had started.

The land, originally a dairy farm, had been owned by the Hewitt family. Just before she'd bought out the practice, it had been subdivided and developed—and the unexpected plum of handling the conveyancing for the developers, the Hewitt family again, had fallen into her lap.

She'd been unable to believe her good luck then briefly disturbed when her father, with whom she'd always had a turbulent relationship, had hinted that he'd been instrumental in getting her this coup. He had, frustratingly, refused ever to elaborate.

But the fact of the matter was that she'd never looked back. Other estates had sprung up as well as strata title unit developments, some litigation work had started to come her way and she'd soon had more work than she knew what to do with.

As a direct result, she now owned her own apartment in a lovely position close to the beach, she drove a magenta-coloured flashy little sports car and, when she could take the time for a holiday, she could afford the exotic and unusual.

But it wasn't until about six months after the plum had fallen that she'd met Lachlan Hewitt himself. She'd always dealt with his project manager although by then she'd known a lot about him and the family history: about his grandfather who had bought up so much of the country for a song. About the macadamia and avocado plantations they also owned; about the wonderful old house they lived in.

Then, one day, when she hadn't even had time to

read through her appointments for the morning, Lucy, her receptionist, had buzzed her and announced in hushed tones that Mr Lachlan Hewitt had arrived for his appointment.

Clare had gasped, gazed around at her littered desk then down at her person, and, in a voice unlike her own, had asked Lucy if she could stall him for a minute or two.

'If you say so, Ms Montrose,' Lucy had replied disapprovingly.

Coming back to the present, Clare smiled faintly as she recalled her receptionist's exact tone. And recalled how she had tidied her desk frantically, smoothed the skirt of her straight taupe linen dress with its white revere collar, reached into a drawer and studied her face in the small mirror of her gilt compact. And she'd had no more time than to run her fingers through her hair, apply a dash of lipstick and smooth her eyebrows before a discreet knock had sounded on the door.

She remembered it as if it were yesterday, she thought, and closed her eyes as the images of that first meeting seeped into her mind...

'Ms Montrose, Mr Hewitt,' Lucy said as she ushered a tall man into the office.

'How do you do, Mr Hewitt?' Clare came round the desk and offered her hand.

'How do you do, Ms Montrose?' Lachlan Hewitt replied, with the faintest emphasis on the Ms and a slight narrowing of his eyes as he took her hand and allowed his grey gaze to inspect her from top to toe.

Clare blinked once. She was five feet ten and not

used to being towered over, but Lachlan Hewitt was at least six feet four. And those penetrating, smoky grey eyes were set in a tanned, interesting face beneath thick tawny hair with a tendency to flop on his forehead. The rest of him was well-proportioned: wide shoulders, narrow waist and more than a hint of whipcord strength beneath his casual checked shirt and khaki trousers worn with short brown boots.

But what surprised her most was that he was younger than she'd expected—in his middle-thirties, she guessed.

The other thing that surprised her was the hiatus that developed as they stared at each other. So that even Lucy appeared to be rooted to the spot.

Clare decided to break it with a tinge of annoyance running through her. She did not appreciate being so thoroughly inspected even by the head of the Hewitt clan, she decided, and said smoothly as she took her hand back, 'Do sit down, Mr Hewitt. May we offer you coffee or tea? It's about that time.' She smiled perfunctorily and moved back around her desk.

'Something cool if you have it,' he murmured.

'By all means but I'll have coffee, thank you, Lucy.' Clare sat down and clasped her hands on the desk as Lucy left. 'I presume you've come to discuss the housing estate with me, Mr Hewitt?'

'No,' Lachlan Hewitt replied idly.

Clare blinked as a pause of his making developed. And felt herself grow restive and awkward as she was once again the subject of his scrutiny. But one of the things she'd taught herself over the years was the value of not rushing in, although, she thought,

with some self-directed irony, she had rushed in initially.

All the same, she managed to make herself wait
with no more than a polite look of enquiry.

'No,' he said again, and smiled briefly. 'From all
reports you've been most competent and professional, Ms Montrose. As your father assured me you
would be.'

Clare felt her hackles rise as so often happened in
the context of her father, but all she did was smile
meaninglessly.

Lucy intervened at this point with a long frosted
glass of fruit-flavoured mineral water and a steaming
cup of coffee. There was also a plate of biscuits and
she fussed a little as she disposed of these. Then she
left them alone, but her whole bearing was pregnant
with curiosity.

Clare stirred her coffee with a ruefully raised eyebrow. And decided to be honest. 'You've caused a
bit of a stir, Mr Hewitt. Amongst my staff and myself.'

He looked fleetingly amused. 'My apologies, Ms
Montrose—'

'The *Ms* is Lucy's invention, Mr Hewitt,' Clare
broke in swiftly, annoyed again by the odd little emphasis he seemed to place on it. 'She thinks it gives
me some kind of mysterious status but I myself prefer to be known as Clare Montrose, unmarried—
never married for that matter—and I don't mind who
knows it.'

'I see,' he said, and grimaced. 'To be honest, Ms
as a title always makes me think of women in limbo
and I'd much rather call you Clare. I'm Lachlan, by

the way, married but soon to become *unmarried*—and that's why I've come to see you.'

Clare's eyes widened incredulously.

'Have you ever handled a divorce settlement, Clare?' he asked.

'Yes. A few. But—' She couldn't go on.

'You're amazed?' he suggested. 'Because I'm divorcing my wife or because I've come to see you about it?'

'Both, to be honest,' she said a touch feebly, and swallowed.

'Do you know my wife, Clare?'

'No, I've never met her, but…well, she—that is to say, I've seen photos of her in the local paper and—heard mention of her.'

She stopped abruptly as images of Serena Hewitt, stunningly beautiful even in black and white, swam through her mind, and then remembered seeing Serena in the flesh one day, in the village, and realizing that her photos hadn't done her justice.

'And you can't imagine anyone wanting to divorce her, no doubt,' he said dryly.

'I didn't say that but—yes, I guess I'm surprised. Sorry. Uh—why me, though? I would imagine you have a family solicitor who…might be more appropriate.'

'I do. I'd rather have fresh blood in this case, however.'

Clare looked at him narrowly. 'If I took this on,' she said slowly, 'I would act in your very best interests, Mr Hewitt, but if you're looking for someone you could hide some of your assets from with a view to cheating your wife, then I have to tell you you've come to the wrong person.'

'On the contrary, Ms Montrose,' he returned coolly, 'I've come to you because you appear to have a remarkably clear brain and excellent legal skills, whereas my family solicitor is getting old and doddery, although we hold him in great affection. He also happens to hold my wife in great affection.'

'Oh.' It was all Clare could think of to say.

'Furthermore,' Lachlan Hewitt said, 'while I'm prepared to hand over to my wife everything she's entitled to by law, I am *not* prepared to be taken to the cleaners, which is exactly what *she* has in mind,' he finished gently but with unmistakable satire.

'I see.'

'Are you a feminist, Clare?' he asked lazily then.

'No more than most women,' she replied coolly.

'That's not quite as your father sees you.'

She bit her lip to stop the crushing retort that rose to mind and said instead, 'How well do you know my father, Mr Hewitt?'

When he spoke it was gravely but she couldn't miss the lurking little glint of humour in his grey eyes. 'Well enough to know that he holds extremely sexist views but, even so, can't help being very proud of his brilliant, though uncomfortably feminist, daughter—although it's something he may never have been able to convey to you, Clare: how proud he is.'

She coloured slightly and looked away. 'I'm afraid my views of feminist and his don't agree,' she said. Then she asked, 'How *do* you know him, Mr Hewitt?'

'He and my father were great friends. They served together in the same regiment in Vietnam, didn't he tell you?'

'Yes, but I didn't know he knew *you*. I believe your father died some months ago?'

'It was at his funeral that your father mentioned you.'

'I see. Then you mustn't have minded the feminist tag he labelled me with.'

'I didn't say *I* was sexist,' Lachlan Hewitt drawled. 'And I did happen to know that your father saved my father's life once.'

Clare breathed deeply with some frustration. 'Thus the world turns—on the head of a pin. I have to confess I would far rather have earned your conveyancing fair and square but—' her lips curved into a reluctant smile '—I know how petulant and ultra-feminist that would make me.'

Unbeknownst to her, during the short pause that ensued as they traded rather wry glances, Lachlan Hewitt was discovering himself unwittingly intrigued...

Not, on first impressions, drop-dead gorgeous, he thought, apart from those wonderful eyes. A thin, intelligent face, pale, smooth skin and a tall, very slender but elegant figure. Otherwise nothing stood out; well, he amended, there was that shining mass of dark hair and lovely hands—but no, what was intriguing was her air of composure, uncompromising ethics and intelligence even when she was annoyed.

He said, as the pause drew out, 'You've more than earned it with the way you've handled it, Clare. No matter how many times your father may have saved

my father's life, you wouldn't have still been acting
for us if you hadn't proved your worth.'

'Thank you,' she said simply.

'And have I reassured you to the extent that you
feel you could handle my divorce?'

'I...' Clare hesitated then drew a yellow legal pad
towards her. 'Yes. I presume you know that you have
to register a separation which has to stand for twelve
months before the divorce can be finalized, although
financial settlement can be—'

'Yes. We have actually been living separate lives
for at least that length of time and we have also been
through the required marriage counselling.'

Clare absorbed this. 'Are there children involved,
Mr Hewitt?'

'One son. He's six—nearly seven.'

'Will you be contesting custody?'

'Not unless my wife proves to be unreasonable in
the matter of access.'

Clare bit her lip.

'You have reservations about that?' he asked
coolly.

She put her pen down and clasped her hands on
the desk. 'Only to the extent that legal battles over
custody can most harm the person they're designed
to protect—the child, who may become involved in
a tug of war between his or her parents. And, whilst
it's no concern of mine, I always feel morally bound
to point out that this is one area where both parties
should act honourably and preferably between themselves.'

'I certainly intend to,' he said dryly.

'Good. Then if you're really sure about this,

Lachlan, this is where we start trying to carve everything up—to be blunt.'

She said it lightly but watched him narrowly at the same time. Because, in her experience, although in these days of the cause for divorce having to be no more than the simple breakdown of a marriage, the carving-up process could be as painful and complicated as the old way of establishing guilt, and often gave people cause to pause...

But he said wryly, 'Don't worry, Clare, my mind is made up and here is what's involved.'

Half an hour later she had to acknowledge that he had a razor-sharp mind and the considerable Hewitt empire at his fingertips. Also, that the soon-to-be ex-Mrs Lachlan Hewitt would be very handsomely provided for.

'Well,' she said at length, 'on the basis of what you've told me this appears to be a generous settlement and I don't think there should be much for her to contest.'

'Don't you believe it.'

She looked at him enquiringly.

'She'll contest every valuation down to every stick of furniture and throw in some interesting and highly fanciful claims, I have no doubt. It'll be your job to see she doesn't get away with them.'

'I see.' Clare glanced at him again and felt an odd little tremor run through her because of the glimpse of something cold and hard his words had revealed. But he said no more on the subject of his wife and they concluded the appointment shortly afterwards.

She watched him drive away from her first-floor window, in a maroon Range Rover with cream leather trim, and, although it was no business of hers, couldn't help wondering what Serena Hewitt had done to incur the displeasure of her good-looking, clever husband.

Of course, it could be the other way around, she mused as she let the blind drop, but somehow she didn't think so.

And nothing over the next twelve months caused her to change her mind.

Serena did indeed contest every valuation; she contested the validity of the Hewitt family company and trusts, the ownership of the homestead and all the furniture and *objets d'art* in it. She even contested the ownership of the two Irish wolfhounds, Paddy and Flynn, that she claimed she had bought as pups. And Clare had to fight each claim every inch of the way.

Curiously, the only thing Serena accepted with dignity and reasonableness was the access Lachlan Hewitt should have to his son, Sean, which was virtually unlimited.

But finally it was all accomplished, a divorce was finalized, and on that day Lachlan Hewitt said to Clare, 'Well done, Slim. Can I buy you dinner?'

Her eyebrows rose because, apart from nicknaming her Slim quite early on in the piece, their relationship had been strictly professional.

He observed her raised eyebrows with a faint smile twisting his lips. 'I am a free man now, Ms Montrose, if it's your conscience you're worried about—or mine. Besides, I feel you deserve the best meal and best bottle of champagne I can come up with. You've certainly earned it, that was quite a fight you put up.'

Her lips quivered in suppressed laughter. 'If you must know there were days when I found myself wishing you'd at least give her the damn dogs.'

He laughed softly. 'Paddy and Flynn are as big as small ponies. How she planned to have them in an apartment in Sydney makes the mind boggle.'

'In that case I accept, Mr Hewitt,' Clare said after a moment's thought.

And, having never discussed his ex-wife, Serena, personally, that was the last mention he made of her.

They had dinner that night, then again a month later.

It was on this occasion that he said to her, 'I'd like to see you again, Clare.'

She looked across the candle at him, her aquamarine eyes slightly wary.

'But only if that's what you would like. You see, whilst I thought it was inappropriate at the time to tell you this, you've been on my mind in a certain way for many months now.'

And he looked at her with a clear question in his eyes.

Clare found herself breathing a little raggedly as she recalled the many times over the past months when she'd had to admit to herself that she was attracted to this man, and had wished quietly that he was not a client, not a divorcee. Times when she'd lain in bed at night with the sound of the sea rhythmically bathing the shore so close by, and wondering how he saw her.

'I,' she said slowly, 'have had the same problem at times.'

He looked faintly wry. 'Then you hid it well.'

'It would have been unprofessional to do otherwise. For that matter, so did you.'

He grimaced but didn't answer directly. 'Your career means a lot to you, doesn't it, Clare?'

'Yes.'

'Is that why you're looking a little troubled and wary?' he said gently, and slid his hand over to cover hers.

'No. I suppose I'm surprised for one thing.' Her fingers trembled beneath his. 'I'm not terribly experienced for another.'

'You shouldn't be surprised. In your own quiet way you're—captivating. And we know each other pretty well now.'

'In some ways,' she agreed.

'Walk with me along the beach?' he suggested.

The beach was only across the road and she agreed. They took their shoes off and paddled in the shallows, Clare holding the skirt of her long floral dress up. Then they sat on a bench on a grassy promontory and watched the lights of a big ship as it slid up the coast, and the flash of the Byron Bay Lighthouse.

To her surprise, they talked. He told her about his great-grandfather and how he'd come to Australia with only a few pounds in his pocket. He talked about his son, Sean, who was now seven and had a very high IQ and an equally high propensity for getting into trouble, and about how his latest crop of macadamia nuts was progressing.

And she responded, gradually relaxing and telling him about her teenage years when her fascination with law had begun to emerge, her years at university and something of her home life. She'd grown up in Armidale, a leafy, pretty town of some substance on the tablelands of New South Wales about three hundred and seventy kilometres south of Lennox Head. Armidale was home to the University of New England and home to her father's prosperous tractor and farm machine agency.

She told Lachlan that she was an only child, and something about her gentle, retiring mother. Also, how her father dominated her mother and had tried to dominate her.

'Which fed your ambition, I suppose,' he commented.

'Probably,' she agreed with a little grimace.

'Helped along by being as bright as a tack, no doubt.'

'That hasn't always been an asset,' she said slowly.

He put an arm around her shoulders. 'Frightened all guys away, you mean?'

Clare hesitated because she was suddenly acutely conscious of him, but she tested it in her mind, this first physical contact. And came to the conclusion that she felt comfortable against him, that she liked the subtle scent of clean cotton and his faint lemony aftershave, and even wished to draw closer to his warmth and bulk.

'Perhaps,' she answered eventually. 'Not that it's ever bothered me greatly,' she added honestly.

'It hasn't frightened me away—it's part of the attraction,' he said quietly. And he started to kiss her for the first time.

Initially she was aware that the feel of his fingers

moving gently on her cheek was pleasant. That his lips were cool and dry and she seemed not to mind parting her own for him. Then her senses took over.

The hunger that she'd battened down for twelve months asserted itself and the intimate act of being kissed by a man became a mutual pleasure.

The difference between her own soft skin and the slight graze she felt as she trailed her fingertips along his jaw, the knowledge that he could probably span her waist in his long, strong hands—all this brought a heady feel of elation and desire.

The feel of his arms around her, the feel of him against her body was rapturous and ignited a steady flame within her that made her forget the beach, the bench, the park. It was as if the only beacon in the night was this man and the mixture of excitement and quivering need he aroused in her...

When they drew apart, Clare was stunned and speechless for a few moments. Then she said, 'I didn't expect that...'

He grinned. 'That we would generate those kind of fireworks? I did.'

Two weeks later they became lovers.

Coming back to the present again, Clare moved restlessly in her office chair and put her hand on her stomach.

It was six months since she'd begun a relationship with Lachlan Hewitt. Six months during which she'd been—well, almost blissfully happy, she conceded to herself. Six months during which the power of their attraction still took her by surprise.

He still called her Slim, but he used it now in

moments of great intimacy, when her slender figure with its pale satiny skin fascinated him and together they experienced the kind of passion she'd thought might never exist for her.

Then there was the friendship they enjoyed, the moments of laughter, the things they did together such as climbing to the top of Lennox Head and watching the hang-gliders take off. But there were no ties—she still worked as hard as ever and if she wasn't available he never made a fuss, and vice versa.

She visited Rosemont, the family home, often, and knew young Sean as well as Lachlan's aunt May who ran the house, and Paddy and Flynn who *were* the size of small ponies but otherwise charming and gentle dogs.

By mutual, unspoken consent, she never stayed at Rosemont, however, although Lachlan stayed often at her apartment. But she didn't feel excluded by this; she wouldn't have felt right about it anyway.

Yet there had been times, she mused, still with her hand resting gently on her stomach, when an unidentifiable sense of unease had troubled her. How strange that an unplanned pregnancy should crystallize it all, she thought suddenly, and sat up.

She picked up her pen to doodle absently on her blotter and asked herself some things that she should have asked months ago; where had it all been leading, for example?

Had that inexplicable sense of unease grown because she, paradoxically, had wanted more than this undemanding relationship that she'd *thought* so suited her career? How would she feel if he ended the affair—perhaps she'd been a stopgap while he rebuilt his life after Serena?

And, of course, the sixty-four-thousand-dollar question, she mused as she drew a dollar sign on the blotter: what really happened with Serena to make it all go so terribly wrong?

She put her pen down and contemplated the unlikelihood, if she'd been asked to forecast it, of Clare Montrose getting herself into this situation. Because she'd never been able to visualize herself getting deeply, emotionally tangled with anyone. But then again she'd never visualized herself having this kind of relationship with a man, she reflected. Was she mad?

Because even without this complication she knew she was deeply and emotionally tangled up with Lachlan Hewitt, although she might not have cared to admit it. The crunch was, however—and she flinched as she acknowledged it—she had no idea where she stood.

She did have a week, though, she thought suddenly, to really think this through while he was in Sydney on business.

Her phone buzzed and she rubbed her face wearily, knowing her half-hour was up and she was about to be deluged.

But it was Lachlan. 'Clare, can I come for dinner tomorrow night? I'm still in Sydney but instead of being down here for the week I've had a change of plan.'

'Of course,' she said.

'Is something wrong?'

It shook her that he should have been able to read the sudden tension that had gripped her in her voice.

'No, not at all. Well, I'm flat out as usual.'

'See you about seven-thirty, then?'

'Yes. I...I'll look forward to it. Bye!' She put the phone down and closed her eyes. Because her week to prepare her—defences?—had suddenly shrunk to overnight.

And her phone rang again and would keep ringing all afternoon, she knew.

CHAPTER TWO

AT SEVEN-FIFTEEN the following evening, Clare was ready—or as ready as she'd ever be, she thought.

The table was set on the veranda of her first-floor apartment; it was a beautiful evening and the sun was setting. The beach at Lennox Head curved in a seven mile arc towards Broken Head to the north, and the setting sun bathed it in a transitory, golden pink and whitened the surf as it rolled in to a luminous radiance.

In front of her two-storey apartment block, built tastefully like a cluster of town houses with pale grey walls and shingled roofs, thick lush grass grew to the rocks that fringed the water's edge. Immediately to the south, Lennox Head itself rose, clad in emerald-green, to its rocky lip. It was a favourite hang-gliding spot and on weekends provided a colourful, at times heart-stopping spectacle.

The bay formed by Lennox Head and Broken Head was a fisherman's paradise—of the human variety, who fished off the rocks and launched small boats from the beach, and the dolphin variety. It was common to see them in the morning and late afternoons as they curved through the water, flashing their fins.

The village itself was within walking distance, small but colourful with pavement cafés and a holiday atmosphere.

26

None of this was on Clare's mind as she stood before her bedroom mirror and studied herself anxiously.

She wore a long, cool dress in a soft watermelon-pink, gold sandals, and her dark hair was tucked behind her ears to reveal gold hoop earrings studded with tiny pearls.

The dress was loose and cut on a bias so it flowed around her as she moved, and it was perfect for a warm January evening, but she'd actually chosen it for its unrevealing nature.

Not that she could see anything to reveal, she mused. She hadn't popped out in any direction and hadn't put on an ounce of weight.

Then the doorbell rang.

She opened the door—to a dark-suited stranger.

'Ms Montrose?'

'Yes.'

'May I come in?'

'But I don't think I know you,' she said slowly.

'I'd like to remedy that,' he replied expressionlessly.

'Do I have an option?'

'Actually—no.'

'I see.' Clare took an unsteady little breath. 'Then you had better come in.'

He stepped across the threshold and waited while she closed and bolted the door. Then he took her in his arms and murmured, 'It's almost as if you've been waiting for me, Ms Montrose.'

'Not you, someone else,' she whispered.

'I hope I'm able to take his place.' And he trailed his long fingers down the side of her throat.

She shivered slightly. He looked into her eyes then lowered his mouth to hers.

When they broke apart, she was breathing raggedly and he took her hand and turned to lead her into the main bedroom.

She followed after a slight hesitation. The sun had set and a blue dusk was starting to fall beyond her wide windows.

She stood unresisting although she was tense and she kept her eyes veiled as he started to undress her. The zip at the back of her dress went down to her hips and the silky watermelon-pink material slipped off her shoulders. She glanced at him briefly but he only looked narrowly intent as he watched the dress slip farther down. She stepped out of it.

Her underwear appeared to hold his interest for some moments, a beautiful, dusky pink bra with elaborate silver embroidery and a matching pair of high-cut bikini briefs with a tiny silver ribbon bow.

He looked into her eyes again. 'I wonder if they realize, when you're in court and being so very professional, Ms Montrose, how seductive your underwear is?'

Clare licked her lips. 'I don't…always wear… these.'

He smiled briefly. 'Good old Bonds Cottontails for work? Does that mean you wore these especially for the man you were expecting tonight?'

'Yes…' It was the bare echo of the word.

'So he likes you to be sexy and seductive?' He raised an eyebrow.

She didn't answer.

'Or do *you* like to be that way for him, Ms Montrose?'

Again she didn't answer but looked at him proudly.

'Spoken like a true feminist,' he drawled. 'But, on his behalf, I don't believe I should allow this moment to go unrequited.' And he pulled off his jacket and loosened his tie.

But he undressed no further. He took her into his arms first and kissed her thoroughly again before he went to release her bra.

Clare resisted and said huskily, 'Do I have the right of reply, at least?'

'Be my guest,' he invited.

She smiled briefly and undid the knot of his tie and threw it on the bed, and started to unbutton his shirt.

'Ah, that kind of reply,' he murmured.

'Even if I have to do this, I might as well make a statement of my own.'

'Ma'am, I can't take exception to that.'

'Good. How sexy does this make you feel, sir?' Her eyes glinted as she slipped her hands beneath his open shirt and ran them up and down his chest, curling her fingertips in the springy hairs then allowing them to wander down his hard, trim torso towards the waistband of his trousers.

He looked at her wryly but replied gravely. 'More and more so, Ms Montrose.'

Tantalizingly, she let her hands roam up to his shoulders again and eased the crisp white cotton shirt away. The skin of his wide shoulders was smooth and tanned and she bent her dark head and kissed him lingeringly on the base of his throat at the same time as she freed his shirt from his trousers and once again rested her fingers on his waistband.

'May *I*?' he said, not quite so evenly.

'Be my guest,' she whispered, with the faintest gleam of victory in her aquamarine eyes.

They said no more as they dispensed with the rest of their clothing, although she trembled at each touch of his hands on her body—her breasts, the smooth curve of her hips, her inner thighs—and what the contact with his body did to her—igniting her senses and turning her slim, pale figure into an instrument of growing, sheer desire.

Then she was lying beneath him on the wide bed as they came together in a breathtakingly sensual rhythm and, finally, a union that left them both gasping with delight.

'That was a cheap shot at my underwear in court, Mr Hewitt.' She snuggled against him and laid her cheek on his chest.

She felt a jolt of laughter run through him as he combed his fingers through her hair. 'I gathered that—if looks could kill! But you played your part perfectly, Slim. You even managed to turn the tables on me.'

She grimaced. 'You did look like a stranger. I've never seen you so formally dressed before.'

'I went straight to the airport in Sydney from a business conference, and came straight here from Ballina airport.'

'Did you—?' She stopped and bit her lip.

'Tell me,' he prompted gently.

She lifted her head so she could see his eyes, leant

her chin on her hands and said slowly, 'Did you think that after six months we'd still have that kind of effect on each other?'

'I…had no way of knowing,' he said thoughtfully. 'But I can't complain. Can you?'

'No…'

'You don't sound too sure.' He sat up and she followed suit so they were sitting side by side, and he took her hand.

Clare thought for a moment and discovered that her uppermost emotion now was a sense of disbelief. Here she was, a mother-to-be, but indulging in lovely, sensual games—well, to be honest she could no more help herself than fly to the moon, but was it right? Shouldn't she be feeling less sexy and more—what—responsible?

'Clare?'

'I suppose I had no way of knowing either and no, I'm not complaining,' she said humorously. 'In fact, I'm also going to be very traditional and *unfeminist* right now. Lie back and I'll bring you a drink which you can enjoy at your leisure whilst I have a shower and rescue dinner.'

She went to get up but his fingers tightened on her hand. 'We could have a shower together—we usually do—and I could help you to rescue dinner, Clare. Too much unfeminism could have a detrimental effect on you.'

'What do you mean?' She turned to him with a slight frown.

He grinned then said simply, 'I like your brand of independence, Clare. It makes things quite electric between us, or hadn't you noticed? As in—what happened right here not that long ago, for example,' he added softly.

She thought swiftly. 'Ah, but this is just my famed independence in a different form, Lachlan. In other words, do as you're told.' She raised their hands and kissed his knuckles briefly, shot him an impish look, and this time escaped.

But as she showered quickly and donned a cotton housecoat her emotions were different again. This time she felt guilty and a little shoddy because the only reason she'd suggested he relax with a drink was so that he wouldn't shower with her and get the opportunity to study her body in adequate light, just in case there was some tell-tale sign.

He'd have to know sooner or later, she reminded herself. Why put it off? She was scared, that was why, she answered herself. She didn't know how he'd react. She don't know if he'd ever see her as anything other than a tantalizing sexual partner... And perhaps it was the distance they kept from each other, not to mention her famed independence, that kept their affair so fresh and electric.

She'd made curry and rice, one of his favourites, and gone to some trouble with the sambals. He thanked her appreciatively as he studied the feast laid out on the veranda table. He'd showered and changed into a T-shirt and shorts, retrieved from a bag in his car.

It was quite dark by now but the night was starry and the rhythmic flash of the Byron Bay lighthouse could be seen in the sky.

A bottle of wine stood in a pottery cooler but when

he started to pour her a glass she said suddenly, 'No, thanks, Lachlan. I think I'll have—just water.'

He looked at her for a moment then shrugged. She barely drank at the best of times but usually had one or two glasses of wine if they were having dinner together. Would he think something was amiss? she wondered apprehensively.

But all he said, as he poured his own glass, was, 'Big day tomorrow?'

She relaxed. 'They're all big days these days.'

'Ever thought of scaling down?' he asked as they started to eat.

'No,' she said slowly, and then was suddenly conscious of feeling physically uncomfortable, oddly queasy and with sweating palms. 'Uh—but I am thinking of taking on a qualified solicitor.'

'If you did you might be able to spend some time away with me,' he mused.

Her eyes widened. 'Such as?' she asked carefully.

'Well, one of the reasons that I came back early was because I've decided to go to the States in a couple of days. There's a macadamia conference I *wasn't* going to attend but I've changed my mind. I've got one or two other business matters over there so I thought I'd kill all the birds with one stone. We could have gone together.'

'There's no way, at the moment, anyway—'

'There never is,' he said.

She studied his expression by the light of the single fat candle between them, burning brightly in a candle glass, but it was entirely enigmatic.

'All the same it doesn't sound like much of a holiday,' she murmured, and looked at her curry and rice with distaste.

'Oh, I guess we would have found some time to—play.'

Clare blinked as she digested this, and drew no comfort from it, she discovered, as she visualized herself twiddling her thumbs whilst he attended to business matters, and visualized herself being dutifully grateful for the odd 'times' he found to play.

Moreover, she thought, with a tinge of bitterness, she didn't know about this 'playing' any more, even if it was electric and devastatingly irresistible.

She said, with a little movement of her shoulders, 'Unfortunately, even with a partner or an associate, I may only just get back to normal—normal hours, at least, which is not "tripping around the world" kind of time off.'

He finished his curry, pushed his plate away and joined his hands behind his head. 'Oh, well, it was just a thought.'

'How long will you be away?'

'Three weeks.'

Her eyes widened again. They'd never spent that long apart without some kind of contact before. 'A *lot* of birds to kill,' she commented.

'I'm thinking of diversifying—coffee is only a boutique crop around these parts at the moment but it has potential. I'd like to investigate it thoroughly before I go into it, though. If I go into it.'

'Aren't macadamias and avocados enough?' she asked curiously.

'Macadamias suffer fluctuations in world prices, especially since Hawaii started producing and took some of our US market. And avocados can always be tricky to grow. They all can for that matter. It's a good idea to have a few strings to your bow.'

'Well, I wish you luck!' She stood up and began to clear the plates—hers only half-finished. Then she became conscious that he was watching her rather intently, although his smoky grey eyes were unreadable.

'Is something wrong?' she asked uncertainly.

'No,' he said, but after an odd little pause. 'Talking of coffee—'

'Just coming up, Mr Hewitt. Stay there.'

It was just as well that he did, because while she was making the coffee that insidiously unwell feeling gripped her seriously, so much so that she had to dash for the bathroom where she painfully lost what little of her dinner she had eaten.

It had to be morning sickness, she told herself incredulously as she rested her cheek against the cool of the bathroom mirror. But at night? And tonight of all nights—she couldn't believe it.

She waited for a couple of minutes but the nausea seemed to have passed and she cautiously went back to the kitchen. But Lachlan was still on the veranda, gazing out over the sea.

'This is Blue Mountain coffee,' she murmured presently. 'Who knows? I could shortly be serving you Rosemont Premium Blend.'

'Not shortly. It would take a few years, at least.'

They sat in silence over their coffee for a few minutes, Clare sipping hers carefully in case it made her nauseous. Added to this she was in a bit of a whirl as she tried to get to grips with the suddenly tension-shot atmosphere that seemed to have developed between them.

Without stopping to think, she said abruptly, 'Do you ever see Serena when you're in Sydney?'

He looked at her. 'Sometimes. Why?'

'I just wondered.' She shrugged. 'How is it going for her?'

He paused. 'What brought this up?'

'Nothing really. If you'd rather not talk about it that's fine with me.'

'Serena,' he said deliberately, 'is enjoying to the full the jet-setting life-style she believes I denied her.'

Clare blinked at him. 'She didn't enjoy…Rosemont?'

'No. She felt buried alive. So she said.'

'That… No.' She looked away.

'Say it, Clare.'

She took a breath and sat up straighter as a little flame of annoyance licked through her at his tone. If anyone had the right to be curious, surely she did, she thought. 'It sounds to me as if a fuller investigation of your life-style preferences might have been a good idea before you got married,' she murmured coolly.

'How right you are,' he drawled.

She just looked at him.

'But if you'd ever met her you might have understood that at the time they didn't seem to matter—particularly if you were a man.'

'I…I did see her once,' she said involuntarily.

His eyes glinted with mockery—self-directed? she

wondered. He said, 'Then I may not have to spell it out for you.'

No, she thought, and coloured for some reason as she recalled sleek blonde hair, long-lashed cornflower-blue eyes, an aristocratic little nose and lots of smooth golden skin exposed in a mini-dress that did little to hide a sensational figure. Plus, she mused, a definite air of combined hauteur and come-hitherness that would be hard for most men to resist.

'I see,' she said at length.

He smiled unamusedly. 'A very lawyerly comment.'

'Lachlan—' She stopped, and stopped herself from simply saying, *I'm pregnant, Lachlan. That's why I'm curious although I probably always have been. It's my own fault that this happened but—what do you suggest we do?*

'Clare?' he said after a moment.

'I'm tired. I have got a big day tomorrow, that's all.'

He looked at her ironically. 'My marching orders in other words?'

'I didn't say so but if that's how you want to take it, yes,' she said bleakly. 'We don't seem to be…enjoying each other's company much at the moment, do we?'

'There's an old saying about too much excitement and high spirits causing tears before bedtime.'

'Don't patronize me, Lachlan, I'm not in the same league as your seven-year-old son,' she warned tightly. 'Anyway, you started it.'

'He's eight now and you were more than happy to play along. However—' he rose and kissed her lightly on the forehead '—before this gets out of hand and becomes a sordid little "domestic", I'll say goodnight, Ms Montrose.'

He stood over her for a long moment, staring down at her enigmatically. But Clare only gazed back at him mutinously. And he turned on his heel and walked out.

She lay on her bed, dry-eyed but distraught.

For once in her well-ordered life she had not so much as rinsed a dish or removed anything from the table on the veranda. The mere thought of anything to do with food, particularly leftover, cold food, was anathema to her. But the thought of how disastrously the evening had ended was worse.

A sordid little 'domestic', she thought bleakly. But what had really started it? Things had seemed to deteriorate before she'd mentioned Serena. So it went back to his trip to the States, she supposed. Yet he'd never before even suggested they go away together and he must have known a business trip for *him* wouldn't particularly appeal to her—unless he'd decided he needed a more available, amenable mistress?

The thought shook her and chilled her to the bone.

But in line with his obvious distaste for any kind of domestic dispute as well as his clear reluctance to discuss his ex-wife with her, what else was she supposed to think? she asked herself sadly.

And just how would he react if he knew that what she really longed for at this moment was not some jaunt halfway around the world, but to be able to curl up next to him, feeling warm and safe, with no thought of work, no decisions to make other than what they were going to call this baby because *he* had everything else under control?

She sighed and, for the first time since she'd found out she was pregnant, let her mind wander...

A girl? Well, a girl would be ideal, seeing as he already had a boy, but then again Sean might prefer a brother. If she had to do this on her own, though, perhaps a girl would be easier—how crazy was that, Clare Montrose? she chided herself. She had no choice; the baby's gender was decided. And, whatever happened, it was hers...

Valerie Martin popped in to see her a couple of mornings later, a Saturday. She had heard nothing from Lachlan in the interim and wasn't even sure whether he was still in the country.

'How's it going, Clare?'

'I'm not sure,' Clare said cautiously. 'Come in and sit down for a moment. I think I may have started this morning sickness bit but—it was at night and I had had some curry so—'

Valerie laughed. 'Millions of Indian women have curry as a staple diet and morning sickness at night is quite common. Welcome to the club!'

Clare grimaced. 'It just came on out of the blue; it was a pretty lousy experience but once it was over I felt fine again, well—relatively fine. It was also two nights ago and I haven't actually been sick since although...' She gestured.

'That sounds par for the course. By the way, I forgot to tell you that your first scan should be at about eighteen weeks—I can make all the arrangements but if you'd prefer to transfer to an obstetrician I can refer you to one.'

Clare gazed at Valerie Martin, who had four children herself, she knew, and who was assuming the proportions of a lifeline as someone she respected and liked as well as someone who knew some of the background of this pregnancy. 'Do I have to?' she said doubtfully. 'I'd much rather stick with you.'

She paused and contemplated the sudden and alien thought of scans, hospitals, the sheer invasion of physical privacy that was about to descend on her, and paled slightly.

Valerie's face softened as she watched this knowledge come to Clare Montrose, who, she had no doubt, was a very private woman.

She said, 'Here's what we could do. In case, just in *case* of any complications, we could engage an obstetrician to be on standby. I would handle the bulk of your pregnancy—no pun intended,' she said humorously, 'and he would see you a couple of times as well as conducting the ultrasound scans, and be on call for the delivery. That covers all eventualities but it's quite likely he won't be needed.'

Clare relaxed. 'Thanks. Most of this is such new territory for me, I, well—'

'I know. At least, I guessed,' Valerie said.

'I suppose I've been so wrapped up in my career—but—' Clare stopped and shrugged. 'It's not only that. I'm an only child, I don't have any aunts and uncles or cousins—'

'Both your parents were only children?'

'Not really. My mother lost a brother at birth, but that counts as being an only child, I guess. Uh—so

I've never been closely associated with anyone pregnant or had much to do with babies. I lost touch with most of my girlfriends before they had any. I—' She stopped again, then said ruefully, 'I was always a bit of a loner.'

'Have you told him?'

They stared at each other.

Until Valerie said bluntly, 'Forgive me, but if we're going to be friends as well as patient and doctor—'

'No,' Clare said. 'I mean, yes, I would very much appreciate your friendship, Valerie. But no, I haven't told him. I have only seen him once, a couple of nights ago, and—I just couldn't seem to say it.'

'Probably best *to* just say it, Clare.' Valerie shook her head and grimaced. 'Very easy to give advice, however. What about your parents?'

'My mother,' Clare said slowly, 'has always longed for me to marry and have children. So has my father, I guess, although for all the wrong reasons.'

'Most grandparents fall in love with their grandchildren whatever the scenario,' Valerie commented. 'By the way—' she smiled mischievously at Clare '—speaking as your doctor—and you may not like this but I genuinely recommend it—you need to have plenty of rest. I'm all in favour of some exercise but—' she sobered '—the first trimester, Clare, needs some care taken of it.'

'I...I'm going to put a full-time solicitor on.'

'Good girl!' Valerie rose and deposited a package on Clare's desk. 'All you need to know about the course of your life for the next seven-odd months—

what you should do, what you shouldn't, some information on antenatal classes in the area, et cetera, et cetera.'

'Thanks.' Clare grinned and rose. 'I'll make it my weekend project—well, one of them.'

She had intended to work through the weekend although the office closed at noon on Saturday, but as she locked up and stepped out to get herself some lunch, and stepped off the pavement deep in thought, a maroon Range Rover all but ran her over. It swerved wildly and screeched to a halt beside her and it was Lachlan who jumped out.

'What the hell do you think you're doing?' he demanded, his grey eyes furious, his jaw hard as she tried to collect herself and still the pounding of her heart.

'I...I wasn't thinking,' she stammered.

'You could have been killed! Not to mention being instrumental in causing a head-on collision.'

'I'm sorry. I...really am sorry—what are you doing?'

'Kidnapping you,' he said sardonically as he steered her towards the vehicle and gave her no choice but to get in. 'What do you think I'm doing?'

Clare had to hitch up her slim straight skirt to negotiate the high step, and while he gave her no help he penned her in so that there was no chance of escape. Then he slammed the door on her and strode round to get in himself.

She said coldly, although she clutched her hands in her lap to stop them from shaking, 'Considering that I had assumed you'd left the country—I have no idea what you're doing or planning to do.'

'Then I'll tell you.' He shoved the gear lever forward and drove off, spinning the tyres. 'I don't—as you put it with such criminal connotations—*leave the country* until tomorrow. So I'm taking you up to Rosemont for lunch and if you dare say anything about how you'd planned to work this afternoon, Clare Montrose, I shall be even more annoyed.'

She bit her lip, not only at his words but the plain warning in his eyes.

He also said, 'I'm all for being industrious and so on but when it's taken to the heights you do, when it ousts every other damn thing from your mind, then it's about time someone told you enough was enough. It is also Saturday afternoon—and my last day here for a while.'

Clare swallowed. 'I wasn't sure whether…you wanted to see me again.'

He was silent for a moment as he turned onto the Byron Bay Ballina Road. Then he said abruptly, 'Do you want to see me again, Clare?'

Her voice seemed to stick in her throat. But finally she heard herself say, 'I've been thoroughly miserable since…then. And not sure what went wrong. So I didn't really know how to—' she laced her fingers together '—approach you.'

She said it all staring straight ahead as he swung into Ross Lane which would take them up from the flat, coastal plain to the gently undulating countryside around Tintenbar and Alstonville.

Then, to her surprise, she heard him laugh softly,

and her aquamarine eyes were puzzled and questioning as she turned to him.

'Approach me?' he said softly, and put his hand over hers. 'Clare, all you had to do was click your fingers and I'd have come running.'

She gasped. 'I'm sure you wouldn't!'

'Ah, well, perhaps not.' His eyes were amused. 'But I'd have come all the same. The thing is, I don't know how things went so awry the other night either but there's obviously some worm of discontent niggling between us and I'd like to get to the root of it before I go.'

It shot through her mind that the problem between them would not be susceptible to solving in one afternoon, did he but know it.

She said quietly, 'Perhaps we were foolish to think we could live in some sort of time capsule, so—' she hesitated '—untouched by anyone or anything else, for ever.'

'You've always seemed perfectly happy with the status quo, Clare.'

'So have you. And yes, I was. It suited everything about my life so well. But it's not, well, it's not what I imagined could ever happen to me. So I've had moments of—unease.'

'Tell me.'

She shrugged her slim shoulders. 'Will it last? Can a relationship so physically orientated and so determinedly detached in every other respect last? Am I a stepping stone while you get over Serena? Those kinds of thoughts.'

They crossed the Pacific Highway and the Range Rover swept down a winding road then up again to-

wards the lovely, camphor laurel country that was
home to Rosemont.

'That's what was upsetting you the other night?'
he said at last with a slight frown.

Clare took a breath. 'Actually, I was wondering
whether you'd decided you needed a more available
and amenable mistress. To take away with you on
business trips, for example?'

A smile touched his mouth but it was faintly grim.
'Would your unease with our relationship make you
into that kind of mistress, Clare?'

'No,' she said definitely.

'Then I think we have to acknowledge that for
whatever reason—and there are plenty—and despite
the odd bit of dissatisfaction, this is what suits us
best. Yes,' he said as she made a sudden movement
beside him, 'I did suddenly think that I would be
lonely without you on this trip. I did, I don't deny,
think, Why the hell does she have to work so damned
hard anyway?'

'Go on,' she said barely audibly.

He looked at her ironically. 'My next thought was,
I'm sure she'd hate me for thinking along those
lines—and I wasn't wrong, was I, Clare?'

A week ago he wouldn't have been, she mused
sadly. Now? Now, of course, everything had
changed.

'Which is why,' he said at length when she didn't
answer, 'I don't think we should tamper with the
order of things as they stand between us, Clare.'

'I...I was going to say— I see,' she responded as
some inner resource came to her rescue. What she
really felt like doing was bursting into tears, because

the distortions and half truths had established what she'd always feared—that he wouldn't want to marry her. 'But I won't be lawyerly,' she soldiered on with a false smile. 'You're probably right.'

He looked at her narrowly then drove between the white gateposts of Rosemont, only to stop the Range Rover precipitously with a muttered curse as a diminutive American Indian in full war paint danced into its path, chanting and stamping, bending low and waving a bow and a tomahawk.

'*Sean*—that's twice in one day I've nearly run someone down!' Sean's father said explosively.

Clare put a hand on his arm and started to laugh because Paddy and Flynn had appeared and they both wore long-suffering expressions—and feather headdresses tied over their ears.

CHAPTER THREE

'CLARE, Clare!' Sean said excitedly, and jumped into the Range Rover. 'Guess what I am?'

Lachlan got out and opened the tailgate so Paddy and Flynn could come with them.

'An Indian?' Clare hazarded with a straight face.

'Of course!' Sean responded scornfully. 'But what kind?'

'A Sioux? Cheyenne? Apache? No,' she said as he shook his head each time. 'Then I give up.'

'I'm a Nez Percé,' Sean said proudly.

Clare and Lachlan exchanged glances as Lachlan started up the macadamia tree-lined drive.

'I've never heard of them,' Clare confessed.

'They were the greatest,' Sean said enthusiastically. 'Great hunters, riders and warriors until the government took their territory from them in 1877. Nez Percé means pierced nose.'

'I'm glad to see you haven't pierced yours, Sean.'

'I was thinking about it but Aunty May said if I did I'd most likely die of blood poisoning and she'd be the first to dance on my grave.'

'Sean,' Lachlan said, 'if you've been giving Aunty May a hard time—'

'Who, me? Serena sent me these, by the way, Clare.' Sean changed the subject adroitly. 'She may not act like a soppy mother but she sure knows the way to a boy's heart!'

Once again Clare and Lachlan exchanged rueful glances, not only at the sheer intelligence and eloquence this eight-year-old possessed, but his ingenuity and the way he insisted on calling his mother Serena, and treated her, from the way he spoke of her, like a slightly wayward older sister.

May Hewitt was waiting for them on the veranda.

Rosemont was an old federation homestead built on a small rise which gave it excellent views of the acre upon acre of sloping, silent macadamia and avocado orchards that made up the estate. Built around the same time as the Nez Percé got hunted off their traditional lands, it was a whitewashed, sprawling house beneath a huge silver roof with thick chimneys and wide verandas all round. And it was surrounded by velvety lawns and the rose gardens it took its name from.

May Hewitt was Lachlan's maiden aunt, his father's sister, who'd lived all her life at Rosemont, when she wasn't in-house at the famous girls' boarding school she'd taught at, then been promoted to headmistress—a position she'd held for years. Retired now, she was still a dedicated educator and possibly the best springboard Sean's high IQ could have had—although they often lived in a state of armed truce with each other.

Although Lachlan had never referred to it, from the odd thing May had let fall it had soon become obvious to Clare that the reason Serena had been so unexpectedly generous in the matter of access to his son was the simple fact that she found Sean almost impossible to cope with herself.

So, instead of the normal arrangement of a young child living with its mother and spending some holidays with its father, the opposite had happened with young Sean Hewitt, and it seemed to be working to everyone's satisfaction despite the times May Hewitt might feel like dancing on his grave.

'Clare, my dear, good to see you!' May came down the shallow veranda steps and hugged Clare briefly. She was a tall woman with Lachlan's tawny hair now laced with grey, and a wrinkled but fascinating face, full of character. And, despite always looking elegant and groomed, she obviously had a deep affinity with the land.

What she made of Clare and Lachlan's relationship, Clare had no idea; she'd never made any comment, but she did always seem to enjoy Clare's company.

'Hot, isn't it?' she continued. 'We should all be down at Lennox having a swim. Lunch is ready and waiting—Sean, you can't have lunch like that, and would you be so good as to put Paddy and Flynn out of their misery?'

Sean looked all set to take heated issue with this, but Lachlan put his hand on his son's fair head and said, 'Sean, life is full of coincidences.'

'It is?' Sean responded, somewhat distracted.

'Yes. You see, I'd never heard of the Nez Percé until a couple of weeks ago when I happened to read about them in a book that had its background set in the Big Sky country of Montana. You're right, they were the best.'

'Oh, boy!' Sean said joyously. 'Can I read it, too?'

'No, too old for you, mate, but the other thing

mentioned in this book was their spiritual affinity
with wolves, I'll tell you about it while we wash up.'

And father and son went off together companion-
ably, with Sean completely restored to good humour
and full of affection for his father.

May grimaced and offered Clare a pre-lunch
sherry.

'Er—no, thanks. Could I just have something long,
cool and soft?'

'Why not? Sit down, Clare. I've got some barley
water here.'

The table was set on the veranda with an embroi-
dered cloth and napkins in silver rings. There was
cold tongue, potato salad, a green salad, crusty bread
and a vegetable quiche.

Clare accepted a long frosted glass and said humorously to May, 'Are you being left in sole charge
of Sean?'

'Heaven forbid. No, tomorrow I'm taking him
down to spend two weeks with Serena. That should
test her to the limit and bring him back to us more
full of mischief than ever for the last week that
Lachlan's away.'

Clare smiled wryly. 'You could come and stay
with me for a few days. Being right on the beach
might…tire him out.'

Lachlan came out onto the veranda as she spoke.

'The only problem,' May mused, 'is that we'd
have to move his computer down—he's like a bear
with a sore head without it. That's where he found
out about these strange American Indians.'

'I've got a laptop he could use—and two spare
bedrooms.'

Her words fell into a little pool of silence and she realized that Lachlan was watching her narrowly, and May was watching him.

She also realized, as the silence lengthened, that she'd unthinkingly stepped over an invisible line— the line that was drawn between her affair with Lachlan and the rest of the world but especially his family. And she wondered why she'd been prompted subconsciously to do it. Because she liked Sean despite his penchant for mischief and he *was* the half-brother of the baby she was carrying?

Then Lachlan said, 'That's very kind of you, Clare. I'll leave it up to you, May.'

'Well, a little break at the beach wouldn't go amiss,' his aunt said slowly as she looked briefly but searchingly from her nephew to Clare.

'Are we going to the beach?' Sean piped up as he joined them, somewhat less than thoroughly scrubbed of his warpaint.

'Clare's invited you to stay with her for a few days while I'm away.'

'Oh, boy!' Sean clapped his hands joyfully. 'I can fish and surf and watch the hang-gliders, even talk to them—wait until I tell Serena about this!'

'I'm sorry, I shouldn't have done it.'

Clare and Lachlan were strolling amongst the macadamias after lunch. May had declined to join them and Sean had decided to perfect his war dance.

'Done it?' Lachlan queried. 'Why don't we sit down?'

They'd come out into the sunlight beside a bubbling creek and there were a couple of high, flat stones on the bank.

Clare sank down and waved the straw hat May had insisted on giving her, turning as she did so to look back up the slope behind them cloaked with dark green trees in orderly rows. By Australian standards Rosemont was a big estate and when you were on it you couldn't help but be aware of the roots of the Hewitt family, their pride in it and their feel for cultivating the land.

Although Lachlan was educated, cultured and an extremely astute businessman, you only had to walk beside him through his macadamias and avocados to know that his love of the land flowed like a quiet river within him.

Whereas, she thought suddenly, she found these plantations rather eerie, quiet places and she'd never grown anything in her life...

'Clare—done what?'

She turned back to him. 'Invited them to stay with me,' she said.

'Why not? But if you're regretting it, which I can't blame you for,' he said with a grin, 'why did you?'

She looked at him seriously. 'It's not that I'm regretting it. I like Sean, and May.'

'So?' He pulled a long stem of grass and chewed it absently. The sunlight was turning the hairs on his arms to a golden chestnut and there were patches of sweat on his blue-and-white checked cotton shirt.

She looked down at her cream silk blouse and beige linen skirt, at her tights and the thankfully low-heeled polished brown shoes she'd worn to work that morning—it felt like an eon ago that she'd got ready for work—and saw some damp patches on her own blouse.

Then she sighed, repositioned the hat on her head, and said quietly, 'I could see how it took you both by surprise. I felt as if I'd crossed the Great Divide. Then, as soon as Sean mentioned Serena, I realized why.'

'You think Serena would object?'

'I don't know.' She paused a little frustratedly. 'I don't even know if she knows about me but it was almost as if I was disclosing my hand—to May, anyway.' She stopped just on the verge of saying, Whatever my hand is. 'She knows about us? May, I mean,' she said instead.

'I think she would have a pretty good idea by now,' he said wryly. 'But May is not one to pry.'

'Not unless it directly concerns Sean,' Clare murmured.

He shrugged. 'That's perceptive of you, Clare. May would fly to the moon for Sean despite the ongoing appearance of war they maintain. So would I,' he said. 'But she was a godsend when...' he paused '...when life was not all it should have been between Serena and me. But there could be no harm in them spending a few days with you.'

Clare was silent but she thought, As long as *he* wasn't around so Sean would be exposed to her in mistress terms, did he mean?

'Not that it would be very peaceful for you,' he added after a moment.

'Well, I'll leave it up to May,' she said, and was struck suddenly by the thought that if her morning/night sickness continued she might not be able to hide it from May. What was happening to her? she pondered. She never used to act without thinking—was it a symptom of pregnancy? And how was she going to hide anything from anyone before long? That included her staff, her clients, not to mention Lachlan himself.

She took a deep breath.

But he said, 'Know what it would be lovely to do?'

She looked at him.

'Take our clothes off and have a swim.'

'Here?'

'I've swum in this creek all my life. The water's clear and cold, there are no leeches and sometimes, if you're quiet enough and lucky enough, you may even see a platypus.'

'I...if I had a costume, I might have taken you up.'

He laughed softly. 'You could swim in your underwear. Don't tell me you're not hot enough, Slim.' He eyed the perspiration trickling down the side of her face.

'I'm exceedingly hot,' she retorted, 'but there's no saying I mightn't be ambushed by the Nez Percé.'

He chuckled and drew a big, clean handkerchief from his pocket. 'Then we'll have to content ourselves with this.' He soaked the hanky in the creek and handed it to her.

'Thanks.' She took it gratefully and patted her face and neck with it. The rivulets that trickled down from it were deliciously cool and he wet it again and she repeated the process then he did the same.

'That was lovely,' she said.

'So are you.'

She looked up to find that he was staring at her blouse. And looked down to see that the front of it was all wet and moulded to her so that the outline of her lacy bra was visible beneath the thin cream silk, and her nipples had responded to the chill of the water and unfurled into twin peaks, also clearly visible.

A rich tide of colour coursed into her cheeks as she raised her eyes to his, but as she went to stand up he said softly, 'Don't move.'

'I...'

'Humour me just for a moment, Clare.'

She sank back. 'Why?' It came out as a husky little sound.

'Because I want to take this moment with me. So that I can think of you when I'm alone, so slim and grave and lovely. So elegant and classy and—unusually innocent sometimes, even after six months of making love to me. And so that I can at least picture you without your clothes, in the water with me, like a lovely dryad with your hair wet and black, your sea-green eyes so clear and your skin like warm ivory—where it isn't like rose velvet.'

She licked her lips and swallowed as the familiar sensations he aroused in her started to prickle her skin and run through her body.

'You're so slim there are times when I'm afraid I could break you,' he went on in the same deep, quiet voice. 'But it's a joy to me, did you know that, Clare? Because you're also perfectly proportioned and your breasts and your hips are a great trial to me at times. I can't always keep my hands off them without the sternest effort of will.'

'Lachlan,' she said raggedly. 'I…'

But she couldn't go on because he put out a hand to her, drew her to her feet then into his arms. And in the moment before he kissed her he said, 'Think of me when I'm away, Clare. And this.'

How could she not? she wondered helplessly as they kissed passionately.

'Talking of will-power…' as he raised his head eventually and looked down at her, his grey eyes were alight with self-mockery and laughter '…you may have to be the strong one, Clare.'

An imp of humour lit her own eyes. 'Talking of will-power, Lachlan, did you hear that?'

He narrowed his eyes and listened for a moment. 'Ah, how fortuitous—that you have such good hearing, I mean. In all other respects it couldn't have come at a worse moment for me.'

She kissed him briefly. 'I never thought I'd be rescued from a fate worse than death in this manner, Mr Hewitt, but there you go!' She sat down on the rock, arranged her skirt demurely and fanned the front of her blouse.

'There'll be other times, Clare,' he warned with a wicked little glint, and sat down beside her only moments before Paddy and Flynn, once again befeathered, bounded up beside them with a whooping Nez Percé hot on their heels.

The rest of the afternoon was curiously peaceful until Sean dropped a bombshell.

They'd had tea on the veranda and Clare had had

two slices of the chocolate mud cake decorated with cream and cherries, and had thought longingly of a third. Now she was spending a little while with Sean at his computer while Lachlan had a last word with his estate foreman. Only to be told admiringly that she was the one person Sean knew who knew as much about computers as he did.

'Now, that's a real feather in my cap!'

He looked at her assessingly. 'Can I really come and stay with you, Clare?'

'If your dad and your aunt agree.'

'Because I think we get on very well, don't you?'

He had cornflower-blue eyes like his mother set in a thin, vivid little face and his blonde hair stuck up at the crown. 'I do,' she conceded.

'Which could be important if Dad marries you—I haven't said anything to him about it yet—'

'*Sean*—'

'Don't worry, I won't, but I think it would be nice. Mum's got a boyfriend, you see, and they're pretty serious about each other.' He screwed his face up. 'I think he's *ghastly*. He talks to me as if I'm two! But he does have a big house and garden and she asked me the last time I spoke to her whether I'd like to live with them if I could take Paddy and Flynn.'

'What did you say?' Clare asked with a certain fascination.

'That I'd think about it but I was pretty happy as things are. After all, I've lived here all my life,' he said quaintly, as if his life had spanned many years.

'What did she say to that?'

'She said, all the same, it would be much better for me to have two parents around even if one was a step-parent. So I thought, If I've *got* to put up with a step-parent I might as well have one I like and one who could be useful, like this.' He waved a hand at the computer.

'Sean...' Clare stopped, torn between a desire to laugh and a terrible feeling of pity for a child caught in this dilemma.

'Besides,' he went on, 'I could never leave Dad to be lonely and sad on his own. So if he does ask you, Clare, I'd be very happy to be your stepson. And then she couldn't worry about me not having two parents full time.'

And he looked at her enquiringly with those piercing blue eyes.

'Sean,' she said quietly, 'your dad and I haven't...discussed anything like this.'

'Oh, well, if it does come up, at least you know how I feel.'

'Feel about what?' Lachlan asked, coming into the room.

'Shoes and ships and sealing wax and cabbages and kings,' Sean replied pertly.

Lachlan raised an eyebrow at Clare but as she tensed he said merely, 'Ready for me to run you home?'

'Yes.' She stood up gratefully but then she turned and held out her hand to Sean. 'You paid me a compliment earlier, Sean. May I return it? You're the brightest boy I know, and one of the nicest.'

Sean shook her hand gravely, then turned back to his keyboard.

'What was that all about?' Lachlan asked when they were out of earshot.

'A mutual admiration society,' Clare murmured. 'He appreciates my computer skills.'

As they drove through the village, Lachlan looked at her enquiringly. 'Want to be dropped off at work?'

'No, thanks. I'll walk down tomorrow to pick up my car.'

'I'm sorry I can't spend this evening with you,' he said as he drove into the courtyard of her apartments. 'I promised Sean—'

She put a hand on his arm. 'It's OK.'

'Especially—' he covered her hand with his and looked into her eyes '—since we're in accord once again, Clare. Well, I hope you've forgiven me for kidnapping you earlier?'

'I've had a lovely day,' she said.

'But have you?' he persisted.

'Have I...forgiven you, you mean?'

'Yes.'

They stared at each other. And after a long moment she touched her fingertips to his mouth. 'Take care, Lachlan. I'll...be here when you get back.' And she slipped out of the car and disappeared inside.

Lachlan Hewitt found himself gripping the steering wheel unusually hard before he deliberately relaxed and, after a moment's indecision, drove off.

What would it take to pin her down? he thought as he steered the Range Rover through Lennox Head, and pictured her beside the creek—a vision that made him tighten his hands on the wheel again. Perhaps it couldn't be done. Was it a legacy from her domineering father? Did she honestly not give a damn about anything but her career? It wasn't as if he was asking her to marry him...

He paused on the thought then shook his head. Talk about contradictory life-style preferences. Could he see Clare Montrose buried at Rosemont, even though he could never compare Clare and Serena? he asked himself, and smiled with unwanted savagery.

Clare changed into a housecoat and went straight to the padded lounger on her veranda.

A north-easterly breeze had brought the hanggliders out and there were three hanging lazily in the air off the Head. And a fair swell forming long breakers had brought the surfers out in force.

It often amazed Clare—where they all came from and where they went to, how the word was spread—because, be it a weekday, a work day or a wet day, if the surf was good they came. Often but not always long-haired and hippie-looking, often in beat-up old cars or on rusty bicycles with their boards tucked under one arm—a whole alien culture, she mused, with but one aim: to follow the surf.

She sighed and for the first time wished she had only one aim in life—to peacefully and happily bear the baby she was carrying.

Not that she couldn't, she reflected. She was financially secure, she didn't need to depend on anyone, she could virtually do what she liked. But every child deserved a father, so they said. And he was a good father...but the big question was, did he want to be a father again?

Her thoughts roamed back to the creek on Rosemont, to how she'd been on the brink of telling him but how he'd forestalled her and the things he'd said. Lovely and flattering things but they'd effectively stopped her in her tracks. Stopped her from telling him, because if that was what attracted him, she thought, if that was *all* that attracted him, she amended painfully, when she was no longer slim and lissom but heavy and clumsy and undryad-like...who knew?

Besides which, he'd been there and done that; he had a beloved son, why complicate his life? Wasn't that why she might have been a perfect choice as a partner of sorts in the first place? Well, almost perfect. An independent career woman, yes, a definite tick there, an unclinging type, another tick, but perhaps only a B+ for availability—on business trips anyway.

She moved her head restlessly. Then there was Sean, she thought. He was too bright not to know there was something between them that was more than friendship, and he was worried about his father being sad and lonely if Serena remarried—what did that mean?

'Sad and lonely without him or because he's lost Serena?' She said it out loud and realized again just how much Serena Hewitt plagued her.

She went to bed that night with only one thing resolved in her mind—she desperately needed to find someone to share her workload.

Fate, or whatever, found that person waiting on the office doorstep on Monday morning.

'Sue—is it you?' Clare said faintly as she approached her doorway with keys in hand.

'It is I!' Sue Simpson, her only real friend from

law school, hugged her heartily. She was a short, jolly-looking girl who'd had two great ambitions— to be a lawyer and a champion surfer. At the moment she looked like the quintessential surfer with her thick brown hair in a long Indian plait, her skin berry-brown, her clothes nondescript and rubber sandals on her feet.

'How...?' Clare began.

'I just happened to stop in Lennox on my way to Brisbane, Mum and Dad have a beach bungalow here, I couldn't pass up this marvellous surf, and I was walking up the street to get a paper when I saw ''Clare Montrose, Solicitor'' painted on the door, so I plonked myself down to wait for you. My, my, Clare, you have done well! Your own practice! Whereas I'm out of work and down and out!'

Clare laughed. 'Only because you want to be, Sue, I'm quite sure!'

Sue pursed her lips. 'True. I took off for a year's holiday bumming it around the great surf beaches, but my year's up and I desperately need some dosh— you wouldn't have a job going for me? No, I'm only joking, I've got a couple of interviews lined up in Brisbane—'

'Sue, come in, you could be the answer to my prayers,' Clare said slowly.

Half an hour later the deal was struck.

There was no mistaking Sue Simpson's sharp brain and proficiency despite her love of surfing, and it surfaced as they discussed the details.

Clare said, 'I think we should give ourselves a three-month trial period just in case it's not what you're looking for. It'll be quite different from—'

she named some of the big law firms over the border in Brisbane '—but if after three months we're both happy I could offer you an associateship and eventually a partnership.'

'Clare,' Sue said, 'I don't think there's going to be a problem with me being happy. I can live in the beach bungalow, the surf's right at my front door, and it would take me years to work my way up to an associateship elsewhere. Besides, I was born and grew up in Lismore and I know an awful lot of people in the area so I have contacts in the Lismore, Ballina and Byron Shires—I might be able to bring some of their legal work our way.'

'Great,' Clare said. 'But I must warn you I'll be scaling down a little.'

'Don't blame you if you've been running the whole show yourself—getting the Hewitts' business must have been quite a coup. How did you do it?'

'You know them?'

'Lachlan's aunt taught me and terrorized me as my headmistress,' Sue said humorously. 'No, not really, but we've sort of known each other as families ever since I can remember.'

'Oh.'

Sue cocked an eyebrow at Clare. 'You sound a bit reserved on the subject of the Hewitts. I must say I found Serena a bit hard to take. She was always so damn sure she was God's gift to men but otherwise—'

'They're divorced,' Clare said. 'I handled it for him.'

Sue whistled softly through her teeth. 'There you go!'

'There's more,' Clare said, and told her friend the whole story.

'*Clare…!*'

'I know. I'm the last person you could imagine getting into this kind of a muddle.'

'Not…Clare, so that's why you're looking so beautiful!' And Sue came round the desk to give her a warm hug.

Which caused Clare to burst into unlawyerly tears, although she was laughing at the same time. 'You're the first person I've told, apart from my doctor.'

'When are you going to tell Lachlan?'

'When I find the right time and place. I just…don't know how he'll take it.'

'Darling Clare…no,' Sue said. 'I was going to give you all sorts of advice but I'll just say this. You've got a friend on hand now. Is it a boy or a girl?'

'I don't know. I don't think you can know this early, even if you want to, there's not a lot I do know about it, to be honest.'

'We'll look upon it as a learning curve! You didn't pass out top of the class for nothing, Clare!'

The next morning, the spare office in the suite had been made over to Sue, phones et cetera installed, and she was interviewing girls from a local business college for a secretary.

Lucy signified her approval of the new solicitor on the team by saying to Clare, 'Good. I'm glad you got a woman so we're still an all-girl outfit!' Lucy was fifty-five herself.

The three weeks of Lachlan's trip away passed swiftly, much more swiftly than if Clare had not had a friend as well as business colleague to spend time with. He didn't call but she hadn't expected him to and was relieved that she didn't have to make evasive conversation with him.

May rang a week before he was due home to say that Sean had come down with a mild case of chicken pox and would be staying with his mother until he was over it.

In light of Sean's revelation, and despite a sharp little pang of concern for him, Clare breathed a sigh of relief, and she spent an hour searching for an interesting CD-ROM to send down to him in a parcel May was posting.

But she was also relieved not to be confronting May and Sean because she was now almost three months pregnant and there were some signs of it. She was no longer as reed-slim, although with the right clothes it wasn't so noticeable. The right clothes, however, had meant some new ones and a new loose style that could in itself be a give-away.

She'd noticed Lucy eyeing her curiously when she'd gone to work for the first time in a smart blue linen but waistless dress. So far only Sue was aware that she was pregnant and she knew she ought to tell her other staff before they started to gossip—but tell them what? That she was having this baby in some kind of a vacuum?

But the biggest change was in the size and sensitivity of her breasts. Her areolae were darkening and spreading and her breasts felt heavy at times.

Otherwise, she felt well. Her morning sickness had abated although certain foods could reactivate it, but Valerie had told her she was going to be one of the lucky ones by the look of it.

And now that she had Sue and some of the pressure of work off her shoulders she was happy to take long walks on the beach or up the Head, to go to bed early and eat sensibly and to indulge her growing preoccupation with the baby.

She couldn't help it, she was *excited*, she thought once. Her biological clock *must* have been ticking away without her realizing it because there seemed to be a new dimension to her life and herself despite the great problems it might bring her.

Then the day was upon her—one day earlier than she'd expected. It was Saturday and she'd taken the whole day off. It was also close to the end of February, hot and clear.

She went down to the boat passage, an area of calm water on Seven Mile Beach that was protected by a sand bar and much beloved by families with young children because it was so safe. She sun-baked for a while then had a long swim in the gentle swell. There were also babies, toddlers and children on the beach and she watched them with new eyes.

It was as she was climbing the grassy hill back to her apartment that she realized a man was standing on the lawn, watching her—Lachlan.

Her heart started to beat erratically and sheer panic affected her breathing—she hadn't expected him until tomorrow—but she forced herself to go on climbing the gentle slope until they were face to face.

They said nothing for an age because it was almost as if they were drinking each other in through their pores. She thought he looked tired but it was a fourteen-hour flight from San Francisco, which would account for it. His tawny hair flopped on his forehead as it always did and he wore jeans, a navy shirt and had a tweed jacket slung over his shoulder. But even tired, with a curious little frown in his eyes, he took her breath away.

Could he see anything? she wondered with some trepidation as that smoky grey gaze swept over her from head to toe, from the white linen sun hat with an upswept brim to the loose pink shirt she wore over her costume, down the length of her bare legs.

Then he said, 'This is a surprise, Clare, but you look wonderful.'

'Thanks.' She coloured faintly. 'I wasn't expecting you until tomorrow.'

'And I certainly wasn't expecting to find you playing hookey—I called in at the office to be told you wouldn't be in until Monday. Have you actually been lying on the beach?'

'Yes,' she answered ruefully.

'What brought this on?'

'Come in and I'll make you a cup of tea and tell you,' she responded.

He took her hand. 'There's something I need more than a cup of tea but you're right—we'd be better off inside.'

She swallowed and started to walk beside him.

Her apartment was deliciously cool and he threw his jacket over a chair, took her hat off for her and tossed it away and took her in his arms with no preamble at all.

'Warm, like a sun-ripened peach, but also salty,' he teased as he kissed her lightly. 'Whatever has caused this metamorphosis, I'm all in favour of it. Do you know how long I've been thinking of making love to you, Clare? Twenty-three days, four hours and six minutes.'

She couldn't help the gurgle of laughter that rose to her lips. 'I bet you plucked those numbers out of the air!'

He looked injured, then wicked. 'Only to the hours and minutes. Which are ticking by and making life difficult for me,' he added significantly, and put a hand on the top button of her shirt. 'May I?'

She tensed and bit her lip.

He felt it and narrowed his eyes. Then he released her slowly. 'So,' he said, barely audibly, 'things *have* changed. You'd better tell me, Clare. Is there a new man in your life? Has someone swept you off your feet—and taken over where I left off?'

A mixture of shock and outrage poured through her. 'No,' she said intensely with a proud spark of anger in her eyes. 'What do you think I am?'

'Changed,' he said deliberately. 'You always were beautiful to my eyes but now you're like a rose that's opening in all its glory. And you're taking weekends off, lying on the beach—something's happened to you, Clare. Is it true love? It surely has to be something cataclysmic because nothing I ever did produced this.'

She put a hand to her mouth then took it away. 'In a way you did, Lachlan. I…you see…I'm pregnant.'

CHAPTER FOUR

CLARE saw the flare of sheer shock in his eyes and she closed her own and went to turn away.

'No.' He stopped her with a hand on her shoulder. '*Clare*—how long?'

'Three months,' she whispered.

'And you expect me not to be surprised? You've kept this to yourself for three months—*why*?' His fingers dug painfully into her shoulder for a moment.

'I...I didn't know myself until just over a month ago,' she stammered.

'How the hell could you not?'

She swallowed. 'If you remember, I was on the pill—'

'I remember very clearly discussing contraception with you, and you insisting that you would take responsibility for it,' he said.

She set her jaw. 'Let me explain—I know this has come as an unpleasant shock to you—'

'I didn't say that.'

'You didn't have to but please don't interrupt!'

He looked at her sardonically then dropped his hand.

She took a breath and glanced around at her living room with its very pale grey walls, the deep, comfortable rattan suite with floral pink linen cushions, all her treasured possessions—and she told him as clinically as she could how it had happened.

69

'I know it was my fault,' she went on. 'I was warned but I just—I was so rushed off my feet at the time, I didn't even stop to think. It was such a quick bout of whatever bug it was and not that serious, or so I thought.' She spread her hands helplessly. 'Then I realized, belatedly, that my cycle had gone haywire but I had no other symptoms and—'

'You were doing the work of ten people, anyway,' he supplied dryly, 'and once again didn't have time to stop and think.'

'Lachlan, I take full responsibility for—everything. You don't have to worry about a thing.'

He stared at her grimly. 'You seem to be forgetting one thing, Clare. This is my baby, too.'

'I...'

But he went on with a frown, 'Of course, it all falls into place now. No wonder you were suddenly so strange, but why on earth didn't you tell me as soon as you found out? Which had to be before I went away.'

'I...I wanted to think about it. I was...*I* was stunned. And I knew it had to change things between us—'

'You're so right,' he said, and the first glint of humour since she'd told him lit his eyes. 'The sooner we get married the better, Clare. This baby has a three-month drop on us already.'

She put her hands to her face then moved away and sat down shakily. 'Lachlan, we can't just get married like that. You said yourself only three weeks ago that there were so many reasons for us to keep things as they were.'

'Clare.' He sat down opposite her and there was

something big and unusually forbidding about him. 'Don't you think it's a bit unfair to hold things against me that I said when I had no idea what was going on?'

'Basic truths don't alter.' She laced her fingers together. 'We neither of us had any thought of marriage or children—'

'You because of your all-important career,' he pointed out with deadly accuracy.

She flinched but rallied. 'How about you?'

'When you're presented with such an obvious dead end—no, I hadn't really considered it, Clare,' he said evenly, 'but, to be trite but true, circumstances *do* alter cases. And I'm not, whatever else you may hold against me, one for planting a seed then turning my back on it.'

She coloured delicately.

He watched her then said, 'But tell me how you feel about this pregnancy. Shock? Horror? A disruption of your life?'

She bit her lip as she wondered how self-centred about her life and career she must have appeared to him. 'No. I'm daily growing more excited about it. I...' She put her hand on her stomach. 'It's really got me in.'

He stared at her in silence for a long moment, sitting there in her pink shirt with her legs long and brown and bare, and couldn't doubt her as her eyes softened, as her whole aura softened and glowed.

'Has it occurred to you to wonder why?' he said at last.

'Talking of trite but true, my biological clock must have been ticking away without me realizing it.'

'You don't think it could have anything to do with it being *our* baby?'

'Lachlan...yes,' she said quietly, 'but...'

'Then we have good grounds for providing this baby with both of its parents, wouldn't you say?'

She stared at him unhappily. 'An unplanned pregnancy is not necessarily a good reason for marriage, it can quite often be the opposite. It can force two people together for the sake of a child, when they're not suited—'

'We're extremely well-suited in one area,' he drawled, and his grey eyes were mocking as they roamed over her, leaving her in no doubt that he meant how well-suited they were in bed.

Clare set her teeth and willed herself not to be affected by the lazy grace and strength of his tall body beneath the navy shirt and jeans, the way his tawny hair fell, his hands, especially his hands and the memories of what they did to her... 'Perhaps, but—'

'Perhaps?' he parodied with irony. 'I know it's been over three weeks, Clare, but do you remember the last time we made love?'

'Of course.' She moved restlessly and tried to call on all her composure, her years of training and practice. 'There's more to marriage than that, however. As you and Serena must have discovered.'

Something flickered in his eyes. Then he said evenly, 'If you're jealous of her, Clare, there's no need to be. It's entirely over and done with.'

She stared at him, and realized two things—that she was hurt by his first words, and that she was waiting for something, for more of an explanation.

But he said no more and his silence struck a chill chord in her heart because it signified the core of her dilemma: her lack of a real and true insight into the failure of his first marriage and his disinclination to provide her with one, and also the lack of a real and true insight into the man himself.

That was why, she realized, she was gripped by the feeling that she'd only ever been allowed to see one side of this man and perhaps would never be allowed to know his heart and soul.

She also had a strong feeling that the trauma of his first marriage might account for it, or part of it, but the end result was—and it shook her to discover it—that, while she suddenly had no doubt that she was deeply in love with him, she very much doubted and feared his total involvement with her.

She had to doubt it, she thought despairingly. Because if this hadn't happened they could have gone on for years, or until the attraction wore off for him; he'd never given her cause to think otherwise.

She stood up. 'I think, Lachlan, one of the problems is that I may be better suited to being a single mother.'

'I knew your career would raise its head sooner or later,' he said dryly. 'But how do you propose to have a baby and continue to be such a hotshot lawyer at the same time?'

She steeled herself not to take offence at his words or the little flash of insolence in his eyes. And she told him briefly about Sue Simpson without naming her.

'I see,' he said at length. 'You have been busy behind my back, Clare.'

That got through her defences and she said coldly, 'Not at all. It was pure fate that I found her sitting on my doorstep. But she was my one real friend at university.'

'Married?' he queried.

'No—what on earth has that got to do with it?'

'I'm just visualizing you career girls sticking together.'

Her composure crumbled completely, and she was suddenly so angry, she actually went to slap his face although at the last moment she thought better of it.

He watched her calmly then stood up leisurely with a faint little smile twisting his lips. 'Well, we seem to be thoroughly at odds, don't we, Clare? That's a pity, you know, because this second trimester of your pregnancy should be the happiest and the easiest. For example, you'll probably have got over your morning sickness by now—you hid that rather well.'

'So?' she said dangerously.

'And the chance of a miscarriage is greater in the first three months, so that's behind you.'

'I know that.'

'Then did you know this? While you're blooming now, it won't be until the last three months that you'll be really heavy and uncomfortable and plagued by the desire to urinate frequently, possibly have stretch marks and brown pigment forming on your face. Heartburn can be a problem, swollen ankles, the difficulty of finding not only a comfortable position to sit or sleep, but a baby cartwheeling inside you making it difficult to sleep anyway.'

Her lips parted and her eyes widened.

He went on remorselessly, 'Then there's the labour to be got through, and the fallacy for some that because breast-feeding is natural it's easy. More sleepless nights, times when you're so tired you don't know what to do with yourself—that's all in front of you, Clare.'

'You sound like a walking encyclopaedia on the subject.'

'I was the one who used to drive Sean around the property for hours—it was the only way to get him to sleep.'

She sat down slowly, put her hands to her face, and, to her amazement, started to laugh. Then she said softly, 'Oh, Lachlan, you make me feel like such a novice, but—' she sobered and looked up at him '—I still can't just marry you.'

He hesitated then sat down beside her and took her hand.

She said urgently, 'You know what I'm like! And, whether it's right or wrong, it's also the way I'm made. The other thing is, I can't help but know...what you need.'

He raised an eyebrow at her dryly.

'You need—if you did ever want another wife— you need someone who could really share your life. In my own way, I'm as intimidated by macadamia plantations as Serena may have been—you know what I mean,' she said as he moved restlessly. 'I don't share that almost mystical affinity you have with the land.'

'May does,' he said after a moment. 'It didn't stop her from having a career.'

'May was born to it and didn't have a husband.'

There was a short, strained silence. Then he said, 'So what do you suggest we do, Clare?'

'Do?'

'Carry on as before but tell everyone we've decided not to marry—we don't see the need for it, maybe?'

'I...' She bit her lip.

'Or do you have in mind a legal contract awarding me some paternal rights, for example? You know,' he said lazily, 'I seem to remember that you were the one who felt morally bound to lecture me on the subject of how parents should act honourably towards their children.'

She sniffed because she felt like bursting into tears.

'Or had you in mind terminating our relationship entirely?'

He smiled tigerishly as she swallowed, and went on, 'I wonder what everyone would say—that I'd ditched you and left you to fend for yourself? You do realize there's bound to be gossip?'

'If that's why you've asked me to marry you,' she said incredulously, 'I—'

'On the other hand it could be *your* good name on the line,' he interrupted, and shrugged.

She frowned bewilderedly. 'What on earth do you mean?'

'Clare, everyone is going to know whose baby this is. And everyone already knows what a dedicated career woman you are, but even career women have biological clocks—apparently.' He eyed her ironically.

'A-are you saying they'd think I…used you?' she stammered.

'In this day and age when women have agendas that very often feature single parenthood, why not?' he said simply.

She took an unsteady breath. 'Is that what *you* think, Lachlan?'

'I'm tempted to wonder.'

She leant back dazedly. 'You're wrong.'

'Convince me, Clare,' he said softly but lethally.

She was terribly tempted to say to him that what had really happened was that she'd fallen in love with the wrong man! But she resisted it because once she admitted that she would have nowhere to hide, no defences for the hurt of knowing that, while he would undoubtedly stand by her and their baby, he might never love her as she loved him.

Why hadn't she realized what deep water she was in with Lachlan Hewitt? she wondered. Because she was badly hurt already but, incredibly, she hadn't seen it coming.

'I don't know what to do,' she said honestly, at last. 'Other than—'

'You don't want to get married.'

'Lachlan—' she turned to him urgently again and this time she couldn't prevent the tears in her eyes '—this is three lives we're talking about, *four* if you count Sean. We can't afford to rush into anything.'

'I don't think Sean would be a problem, he likes you. And he hates his soon-to-be stepfather,' he added significantly.

'So she *is*…' Clare trailed off.

He frowned. 'You know about Serena's plans to remarry?'

'I...' She stopped and sighed. 'Yes.'

'How?' he asked.

She should have told him sooner; she paused to think. 'Uh...Sean told me. That last day at Rosemont.'

'Why would he do that?' he said slowly, and watched her with narrowed eyes.

She tried to decipher the expression in them and was hit by a horrible thought. 'You don't—you don't think I asked?' she said incredulously.

'Didn't you, Clare?'

'No! He brought it up out of the blue!'

'Tell me,' he invited.

'Oh, hell,' she said hollowly, 'it was confidential. It—'

'This is *my* eight-year-old son we're talking about, Clare.' And now his expression was easy to read; in fact it was clearly dangerous.

Clare rubbed her face agitatedly. 'He told me that Serena had a new boyfriend with a big house and garden and how she'd asked if he'd go and live with them if he could take Paddy and Flynn.'

Lachlan swore beneath his breath. 'Go on.'

She grimaced. 'He told me he thought the boyfriend was ghastly but Serena had said he'd be better off with two parents even if one was a step. And...' she hesitated '...that if he *had* to have a step...he'd rather it was me.'

There was utter silence as Lachlan stared into the distance with a distinctly murderous expression.

'Did you know this?' Clare said shakily. 'That she

wants him back? And *why* does she? I thought it was working out so well the way it was.'

'I knew she was getting married again. I knew she was making overtures to him,' he said grimly. 'I didn't know it was preying on his mind like this.'

'I still don't understand why.'

'Why? I'll tell you. Serena swore she would never have any more children—once was enough, she reckoned. But her husband-to-be may not be aware of that and she could be hoping to placate any fatherly tendencies he might display by giving him a ready-made son.'

Clare gasped. 'She'd do…that?'

'She'd do anything to preserve her figure,' he said sardonically.

'But—'

He glanced at her. 'He's also extremely rich.'

'So are you,' Clare pointed out.

He smiled unpleasantly. 'But I never could abide flaunting it.'

'Poor Sean,' she said, blinking.

'Oh, I know how to fight for my own.' He paused and his mouth twisted wryly after a moment. 'So Sean is quite alive to what is going on between us?'

'Apparently.'

'Well, then, we can cross him off our list of problems.'

She started to say something, stopped and said instead, 'Only if we could guarantee the success of a marriage between us, Lachlan.'

'How can you ever do that?'

She hesitated. 'By not…trying to mix oil and water, for starters.'

'Clare,' he said slowly, 'the difference between you and Serena—one of them—is that she tends to act purely on instinct. Nine times out of ten she gets away with it. She has a certain arrangement of genes plus a kind of sheer vitality and sensuality that can make her instincts irresistible. Until you run up against her most basic one—she's utterly selfish.'

'What are you saying?' Clare asked after a moment.

'I'm saying that I believe where Serena wouldn't take responsibility for her actions when they were in conflict with her ego you would.'

He paused and looked her directly in the eye. 'I'm saying that not only you, but both of us, know where our moral responsibilities lie and we could work together to *make* this work.'

Clare digested that and wondered about moral blackmail but she couldn't deny it was a powerful argument. Unexpected, too. But why would he go to these lengths? she wondered. Because he was a morally responsible man? Would he not have persevered with Serena if he felt so strongly, though? Perhaps he had wanted to, perhaps *she* was the one who broke it all up?

Or perhaps, she thought suddenly, it's all to do with being able to keep Sean out of his mother's clutches...

'I can't think straight,' she murmured distractedly, and made a sudden decision. 'Besides which I'm damp and sandy and shedding it all over the place. Could I just have a quick shower?'

He sat back and shrugged.

* * *

While she was showering she half expected him to come in, but he didn't.

She washed her hair as well and towelled it dry then put on a long, loose cotton knit dress in a colour that matched her eyes, and she gathered her hair back in a silver scrunchie.

When she got back to the living room, she found that he'd made them tea and opened a packet of biscuits. He was sitting at the dining-room table with the tea tray in front of him, talking on his mobile phone.

She hesitated then sat down opposite him. She poured the tea as he finished his call and snapped the aerial of the phone down.

And, as if nothing had changed between them, she couldn't help but do what she would have done normally—raise an enquiring eyebrow at him.

'Ansett,' he said laconically. 'I'm flying down to pick Sean up this afternoon.'

She looked surprised.

'He's over the contagious stage.'

'You'll be exhausted,' she said involuntarily.

'He's dying to come home. By the way, he's thrilled to hear about the baby.'

She put her pretty Wedgwood teapot down with suddenly shaking hands. 'You...you didn't!'

His grey eyes were unreadable. 'Why not? This baby is closely related to him. Far better that he knows about it—just say it's a girl? Not knowing could cause all sorts of complications later in life.' He stirred his tea.

Her lips parted incredulously because this was unanswerable but it also assumed that she was a fool if not worse.

He said then, 'You do see, don't you, Clare, that you're not the only who's involved? Just because you're actually carrying it that doesn't mean to say—'

'Stop it,' she said hoarsely. 'I should have known!'

He raised a wry eyebrow at her. 'What?'

'How hard you were. I saw it during your divorce but this is unbelievable. You're not only treating me like a fool but surely I was entitled to expect that this would be just between the two of us until we came to a decision of some kind? There's so much to discuss, so many factors to take into account, but now you've gone and—' She broke off, breathing heavily.

'Haven't you told anyone?'

'Well, Valerie Martin knows—'

'I wasn't referring to your doctor.'

'Sue knows,' she said. 'Sue Simpson, the girl I hired, I had to tell her—'

'Knows it's me? By the way—' he frowned '—is this the same Sue Simpson who comes from Lismore?'

'Yes... And yes, she knows it's you,' Clare said heavily. 'I couldn't help myself.'

'There you go. These are all small towns basically, Clare.'

'No,' she said intensely. 'Sue won't tell a soul and it's quite different from telling Sean!'

He just looked at her.

'Until...until we know what we're going to do,'

she said unsteadily, and, to her horror, she did burst into tears.

He let her weep into her hands for about a minute then got up and came round the table to her.

'No,' she gulped, but he pulled her to her feet, picked her up and carried her over to the settee.

'Hey,' he said quietly, when he'd settled her on his lap and tilted her chin then lightly kissed her streaming cheek, 'this isn't good for the baby.'

'It's all your fault,' she retorted, then stopped and sighed. 'I mean—I don't mean the baby is—'

'I know what you mean. Right at this moment you hate me.'

'I don't hate you, I just don't know what to do for the best.' She hiccuped then laid her head on his shoulder. 'Well, I do, but you won't let me!'

'Should we put this discussion on hold for a while?' he suggested, and stroked dark tendrils of her damp hair behind her ear.

'What else can we talk about?' she asked bleakly.

He looked down at her wryly. 'Have you had a scan yet? Or is it too early?'

'Yes, about eighteen weeks, Valerie said.'

'That's right. What about an obstetrician?'

She told him the arrangements she'd made. 'I...I feel comfortable with Valerie. To be honest, the thought of hospitals, labour wards, obstetricians and so on makes me a little nervous.'

'I don't blame you.'

'I've never been in a hospital in my life, as a patient,' she confessed.

He smiled and it crinkled the corners of his eyes in a way that always fascinated her. 'They're quite modern about these things now. They even call them birthing centres, some of them, so you don't feel as if you're in such an alien, traumatic environment.'

She thought for a bit then said honestly, 'I'm also a little intimidated by, well, to be honest, how little I know about it all. Less than you, even.' She smiled faintly. 'It's as if I got to twenty-seven ignoring a very basic part of me. And the other surprising thing is I've never had the least desire to coo over babies, yet—' she rubbed her stomach gently '—I've kind of got pretty wrapped up in this one and it isn't even moving, let alone born yet.'

He put his hand over hers. 'Give it another month and it will be starting to move.'

'There you go again—is there anything you don't know about pregnancy?' she asked whimsically as he started to rub her stomach very gently and it felt wonderful.

'Of course,' he said quietly. 'I can never know exactly what you go through, but I do know that you don't have to do it alone.'

'Lachlan,' she said huskily as they stared into each other's eyes, and she stopped as she became aware of how close they were and how safe she felt, how warm and protected, and suddenly her eyes were agonized. 'I'm still not *sure*.'

'All right, let's not fight about it. But is there any reason for us not to do this?'

She blinked.

The way he kissed her was unusually tender. He released her hair from her scrunchie so he could run his fingers through it and stroked her face and neck, to start with, and gradually teased her lips apart.

Then, as always, things started to run away with them, and when they finally drew apart she was quivering with desire and could see it reflected in the heavy-lidded way he was watching her.

But she was also troubled. 'I don't think…' She unwound her arms from his neck, sat up and fanned her face with her hand. 'Um, I didn't think I would feel this way, *should* feel this way,' she said unevenly.

A gleam of amusement lit his eyes. 'Why not?'

'This is going to sound silly but I'm not sure if it's proper—I knew it would sound silly,' she said hollowly.

'Proper? Because we're not married?' he queried gravely.

She bit her lip. 'Proper for someone increasingly into maternity.'

'Clare.' He reached for her and was laughing but there was something else in his eyes, a little glint of wonderment, she thought, but couldn't be sure. 'You are amazingly naive at times. It's perfectly proper— No, I'm not going to go any further,' he said as she tensed a little. 'At what cost you'll never know.'

He stopped and waited as she relaxed slowly. 'It's all to do with what I was telling you earlier, my sweet innocent. This middle trimester in other words.'

'Oh.'

'Uh-huh. It should be a golden time for husbands and wives.'

'I see. Of course, if I'd stopped to think about it, I would have realized that,' she said ruefully. 'Not that my first trimester stopped me from…' She paused and put her hands to her suddenly hot cheeks.

He laughed and kissed her lightly. 'You were sensational.'

'Don't remind me—as a matter of fact that was the first time I had morning sickness, at night.'

'If only I'd known.' He looked at her, suddenly quite serious.

'Are we—' she clasped her hands nervously '—getting back onto…what to do?'

Something flickered in his eyes then they became enigmatic. 'Unfortunately, I have to go. My plane leaves in an hour. But I'll be back tomorrow. I've got the feeling my thinking is not going to change, however.'

'Lachlan—'

'Clare,' he said quietly but determinedly, 'if you don't know what we've got going for us, then you must be blind.'

And he lifted her to her feet and stood up.

She opened her mouth to ask him if he and Serena hadn't had the same thing going for them once but what had that proved? Some instinct made her leave it unsaid, though.

He watched her for a long moment, taking in the new outline of her figure beneath the thin cotton knit of her dress, the gorgeous mass of her hair, her troubled eyes.

A smile touched his mouth. 'I won't be able to call you Slim for a while,' he murmured, kissed her and added as he picked up his jacket, 'I'll see you tomorrow.' Then he was gone.

*　　*　　*

Why didn't she just do it? she asked herself in the middle of the night. Say this was a legal tangle between two other people and she was adjudicating. What would she do?

She would add up the pros and cons and point out where the balance lay. So—pros. He was a good father. There could only be assets for a child born into the Hewitt family, not only materially but in what they would inherit in the sense of family, history and worth. Especially for a child who inherited its father's love of the land.

And all that, she mused silently, has got to beat having a single mother. But say, just say she did feel stifled at Rosemont, that she wasn't the kind of wife he needed, that he had been pitch-forked into this position because of Serena's machinations? Having a wife whom Sean *liked* to bring to Rosemont—the family home the boy obviously loved—it had to strengthen his hand against Serena.

She turned over restlessly and thought that this baby couldn't have come at a better time if that were so, but it wasn't much help to her.

The phone rang on her bedside table and she started up with her heart racing. It was her mother to say that her father had had a heart attack and could she come straight away.

Armidale was a four-hour drive from Lennox Head and she made it just as dawn was breaking. She'd thrown a bunch of clothes into a bag. Instead of waking Sue or Lucy in the middle of the night, she'd left a message on the office answering machine to the effect that she'd been called away suddenly but would be in touch or they could get in touch with her on her mobile.

As she drove through Armidale to the hospital, she was struck by the very clear memory of her mobile phone still sitting on her kitchen counter next to the battery charger stand.

'Damn,' she muttered. 'Oh, well, there's nothing I can do about it.'

And all thoughts of work faded anyway, during that long day as her father fought for his life, and her mother retreated into a shell-shocked little world of her own.

But the next morning, although still critical and in Intensive Care after a bypass operation, he was pronounced stable and the prognosis was hopeful.

Clare took her mother home to the comfortable house she'd grown up in and put her to bed. She thought then of ringing work but was so tired herself, she lay down with the phone right beside her and fell asleep immediately.

There was further improvement when they visited Tom Montrose that afternoon, and Clare's mother started to come out of her trance. They spent a few hours with him then drove home through the leafy streets of Armidale, stopping to buy a pizza on the way.

'He'd be horrified,' Jane Montrose said as they sat down to eat it at the kitchen table. It was cool, much cooler than down on the coast, as the evening drew in.

'I know.' Clare grinned. Any kind of take-away food was anathema to her father—one of the many tiresome stances he took in life. 'Mum,' she said suddenly, 'why do you let him walk all over you?'

Her mother sighed. 'He's that kind of man and I'm that kind of woman, Clare. I think I was born docile and domesticated and to be honest, although I know how much it's infuriated you, I've always understood that it's his basic insecurity that makes him the way he is.'

Clare blinked.

'So, while there are times when he can be impossible, we have a very close relationship. And now,' Jane went on, 'it will be my turn to be the strong one both outwardly and inwardly.'

Clare stared at her then said softly, 'Forgive me, I never understood.'

'I know.' Jane smiled. 'Marriage is a strange thing, what works for some doesn't work for others but one thing I do know—you have to work at it. You have to take the good with the bad, you have to cherish the good and thank your lucky stars because the bad could be so much worse. For example, your father has never looked at another woman and he would be absolutely lost without me, as I would be without him.'

Clare herself was lost in thought for a long moment as it struck her that this was reality and responsibility her mother was talking about. Not the version of love and marriage that told you you could walk out of it when the going got tough. Not the version that took vows but took them lightly... Then she stood up to pour the coffee that was bubbling on the stove.

Her mother said softly, 'Clare, are you pregnant, my dear?'

She all but dropped the coffee pot and looked down at herself in her baggy, fleecy-lined tracksuit. 'H-how can you...tell?' she stammered.

'Darling, I *know* you. You're my only child. And because you haven't been able to tell me I know that there must be some problem.'

The phone in the hall rang and her mother sprang up to answer it. But she came back almost immediately. 'It's someone called Lachlan Hewitt for you. Do you want to speak to him?'

'I...yes,' Clare said, and swallowed.

'Lachlan,' she said into the phone a few seconds later, 'I'm sorry but my father had a heart attack.'

'And you didn't think to let me know?' His voice was grim down the line although he went on immediately, 'I'm sorry to hear it, I hope he's recovering, but do you realize, Clare, that we've all been wondering whether you'd been run over by a bus? Your mobile doesn't answer—'

'That's my fault, in my rush I forgot to bring it. Look, I really am sorry but he nearly died, although he is recovering now.'

'Oh, hell,' he said down the line. 'Now I feel like an absolute heel. Are *you* all right?'

'I'm fine but, Lachlan— By the way, how did you find me?'

'It was the only place Sue and I could think of to at least make a start. Fortunately there aren't many Montroses in the telephone book.'

Clare bit her lip.

'You were going to say?'

She cleared her throat. 'I've decided to stay with my mother for a couple of weeks—at least until he's up and about again. Um—I'm sure Sue can cope and anyway now that the crisis is over, hopefully, I'll be able to communicate with her.'

There was a little silence, then he said, 'What about me? I'd like to come down.'

'I don't think that would be a good idea—he doesn't know about us or the baby and it mightn't be the best time to…confront him with it.'

'Clare…' he paused and his voice was grim again '…is that the only reason?'

She hesitated and sighed. 'No, it will give me a little breathing space, I guess.'

'Or time to decide whether to do a flit?' he suggested dangerously.

She swallowed her sudden annoyance. 'That isn't how I operate, Lachlan,' she said coolly.

'Spoken like Clare Montrose, LLB, but you've shown a distinct tendency to want to do a flit from me in one form or another, Clare. Tell you what— I'll do a deal with you. I won't complicate matters for you on the home front until your father is really well again if you give me a promise you'll be back within a fortnight.'

She breathed heavily.

'Otherwise I'll come and get you, Clare,' he warned. 'The other part of the deal is that you keep in touch.'

'This is ridiculous,' she said heatedly.

'Take it or leave it.'

'But I'm not your prisoner!'

'No, you are the mother of my child, though.'

'And a very annoyed one at this minute, I have to tell you!'

He laughed softly. 'I'll make it up to you when I see you again. Promise me one other thing—take care.' And he ended the call.

'Well,' Jane Montrose said, and covered her daughter's hands with her own as Clare sat down looking dazed, 'I think you'd better tell me about Lachlan Hewitt. I've got the feeling he just could be the father of my first grandchild.'

During the next two weeks, Clare and her mother were very ordinary. Jane Montrose, after having expressed the opinion that Clare should take up Lachlan's offer of marriage, didn't labour the point, and added that whatever happened she would be behind her every step of the way.

Then she took Clare shopping and they came home laden with white wool and all the makings of a layette.

It turned out to be good therapy for Clare, who remembered that she'd inherited her mother's skill in that area although it was years since she'd done any sewing or knitting. And it kept them occupied for the two weeks that Tom Montrose was in hospital, as well as being a time on their own together during which they got to know each other as adults and which was very special to them both.

She rang Lachlan every couple of days and when the two weeks was all but up told him she needed an extension to be on hand for the first few days her father was home.

And, at her mother's quiet insistence, when Tom

Montrose had been home for three days, they told him together.

His reaction astounded his daughter. He got sudden tears in his eyes and asked if he could have his name included if the baby was a boy. On the subject of her unmarried state he looked philosophical although, unbeknownst to Clare, he was on the receiving end of an almost militantly warning look from his wife.

On the subject of who the father was, he again surprised Clare. 'Well, well,' he murmured, 'from little acorns oak trees do grow, after all!' But he refused to elaborate.

The only thing that was not resolved during her stay with her parents was what she would do when she got back.

But as she hugged her mother and said goodbye Jane patted her stomach.

'I know,' Clare laughed, 'I'm popping out all over!'

'Clare—' her mother frowned suddenly '—when you see your doctor next, there's something I think you should mention.' And she told her what it was.

CHAPTER FIVE

'THIS can't be happening to me,' Clare said helplessly to Valerie Martin.

'I'm afraid it can, Clare.' And the obstetrician conducting the ultrasound scan agreed. 'See, there's no doubt.'

They'd brought the scan forward because the first thing Clare had done when she'd got back to Lennox Head, even before she'd seen Lachlan, gone to the office or gone home, was visit her doctor. And Valerie had immediately rung the obstetrician and begged for an appointment then and there. She'd insisted on coming and driving Clare herself.

Clare stared at the monitor she was hooked up to via a pad on her stomach and felt like fainting.

'What's more, we'll print you a picture or you can have a copy of the video,' the obstetrician said. 'But we'll certainly have to watch you more closely now—er—Ms Montrose. Especially in light of your mother's history.'

'You can get dressed now, Clare,' Valerie said kindly. 'It's lucky it's a slow day for me, I can shout you lunch and we can talk about this.'

But despite all Valerie's reassurances that this could be handled Clare was still feeling like fainting when she let herself into her apartment. Five minutes later, Lachlan arrived.

She opened the door to him and they simply stared at each other for a long moment.

Until he said quietly, 'I've missed you, Slim.'

'I'm not slim and I may never be again,' she said jerkily.

His grey gaze roamed up and down her figure. 'Yes, you will. In the meantime, it can be a private joke between us.'

'You don't understand.' She stopped and took a breath. 'Come in.'

He came in and took her in his arms. 'How is he—your father?'

'He's doing fine,' she said but distractedly.

'Does he know he's expecting his first grandchild?' He kissed her lightly.

'Not—yes, he does. He was amazingly good about it, they both were.'

'So—' he frowned faintly and watched her for a moment '—what's wrong? Are you trying to tell me something?'

'Yes—'

'I'm not going to go away, Clare,' he warned deliberately, 'whatever you may have cooked up with your parents.'

'It's not that,' she said, and closed her eyes. 'Lachlan, my mother was a twin!'

'A...' He paused then said, 'Perhaps we should sit down.' He led her into the lounge, and they sat down side by side on the settee. 'Go on.'

'Well, I suppose I knew about it but I'd forgotten. I did know she had a brother who'd died at birth, it just—never occurred to me to think of the significance that he was a twin. But, while anyone can have twins, your chances are much greater—'

'If it's in the family,' he said slowly.

'Not necessarily. If my father had been a twin it wouldn't have mattered—it comes down through the maternal line, you see, and—'

'Clare, the suspense is killing me—are you telling me we're *having* twins?'

'Yes,' she said tragically.

To her utter amazement he started to laugh.

'You don't understand!'

'Oh, yes, I do. Whilst a single parent of a *single* baby might be viable, twins could be another matter altogether, Ms Montrose.'

She stared at him, full of frustration and all sorts of feelings she couldn't begin to name, because he'd hit the nail on the head, although not all the nails.

'It's not funny,' she said. 'And that's not *all*! I was starting to love this baby, I was full of plans and affection for it and— But now there are *two* of them—and all you can do is laugh, as if you're having the last laugh to make matters worse!'

He sobered as he watched the expressions of bewilderment, shock and outrage chase through her eyes.

Finally, he put his finger under her chin. 'Clare Montrose,' he said softly, 'whatever else I may be guilty of, I have no problems with twins—our twins. But this is going to be a little harder for you and for that reason alone, although there are plenty of others, I am *not* going to walk away, so you may as well get used to the idea.'

'Lachlan—'

'No, Clare, it's not a question of will you marry me any more, but quite simply when?'

They were married ten days later.

It was a simple ceremony at the church in Armidale where she'd been baptized and confirmed.

The bride wore a pale, lustrous grey silk suit, tunic-style, with short gloves and grey kid shoes. She carried a bouquet of the palest pink rosebuds and around her neck she wore a single string of rosy pearls with a pink Argyle diamond clasp—her wedding present.

The groom, when she turned to glance at him as she joined him at the altar, all but took her breath away—an effect he'd had on every female present whatever their age. He wore a beautifully tailored charcoal suit, his tawny hair was tamed and thick and he was so tall and distinguished, Clare felt a tremor run through her, but not only because of that.

There was a little glint of something in his smoky grey eyes as they rested on her that was electrifying. So much so that she didn't dare to look at him directly again.

They had no attendants other than Sean, who stood at his father's side in his first suit, obviously excited and happy as well as scrubbed within an inch of his life, although nothing had prevailed to make his fair hair lie down on his crown.

All her staff had come down for the wedding, May was there as well as Valerie Martin, and her parents were plainly delighted. Even Paddy and Flynn, waiting gravely on the church porch, had little silver bells entwined in their collars.

But on the first night of their honeymoon, as they stood in the middle of their bedroom on a lovely tropical island off the coast of Queensland, Clare felt unsure and tense.

They'd flown to Townsville then boarded a small sea-plane for the short flight north to Orpheus Island. Situated in the Palm Islands, the resort on Orpheus faced the sheer majesty and breathtaking scenery of Hinchinbrook Island. Hinchinbrook, separated from the mainland of North Queensland by a narrow channel, was world-heritage listed for its unique beauty and pristine environment.

But what she'd seen of Orpheus was lovely, too. Small and exclusive, the resort faced a white beach and sparkling waters with the bulk of the island rising behind it, grassy and golden. As they'd landed the sun was setting and the Palm Islands had floated almost ethereally in a violet sea while the sky over the mainland glowed a fiery orange.

They'd had dinner almost as soon as they'd landed and that had been easy. Pleasant company, wonderful food, a starry, warm night.

But instead of feeling relaxed Clare knew she was feeling the opposite. So much had happened in the last ten days it was hard not to feel shell-shocked, she reasoned. And Lachlan had orchestrated it all. So smoothly, she marvelled.

He'd taken all the embarrassment out of revealing her pregnancy to her staff by presenting them with a *fait accompli*. He'd come into work with her the next morning and announced not only their impending matrimony but the news that they were expecting twins in late August. Everyone had been delighted.

He'd sent a notice to the newspaper to the same effect and before long Clare had been receiving calls of congratulations from clients. He had, she was sure, connived with Sue to make sure the day-to-day burden of running the practice was eased off Clare's shoulders. He'd even come up with a third-year articled clerk desirous of moving to Lennox Head, whose articles they'd been able to take over.

And he'd taken her to Rosemont several times and told her she could rearrange the homestead however she liked. They'd decided to keep her apartment as a retreat on the beach.

But as she'd walked through the rooms of her new home she'd felt like pinching herself and something else—a sense of disbelief that this was going to be her home from now on. Even May's quiet but sincere words of genuine welcome hadn't taken that away.

The one thing he hadn't done was make love to her. They'd not spent that much time alone in fact, for several reasons, the foremost being that the macadamia-picking season had just commenced. The nuts began to fall towards the end of March generally and his had been right on cue, so the harvest had begun and he'd had a lot of things to organize so that he could be away for the week of their honeymoon.

But the other thing that troubled her as they stood facing each other was the memory of that glint in his eye as they'd looked at each other in the moments before their wedding had begun.

Electrifying, yes, she thought, but something else—had there been a gleam of triumph?

'Clare?' he said quietly.

She moved. She'd changed into slim white stretch trousers and a loose yellow overblouse with white flowers on it—she'd again had to acquire a new wardrobe.

'Too big a day?' he murmured, and put his hand on the nape of her neck to massage it gently.

She moved again, luxuriously this time, as his slow-moving fingers seemed to work magic on some of her physical tensions. 'I don't know. I'm not sure how I feel.'

'Kidnapped?' he suggested.

Her eyes widened. 'How did you know?'

'I know you better than you think. By the way, you were a stunning bride.'

She grimaced. 'A pregnant one.'

'No one seemed to mind, least of all me.'

'I thought you looked...' she paused '...triumphant.'

He didn't ask her when or why. 'I was.'

She blinked.

He laughed softly. 'Didn't you think I'd admit it—or have any right to be?'

'It doesn't sound—very civilized.'

'I don't feel very civilized. To be perfectly honest, Clare, when I saw you next to me in the church, looking so lovely, so wary and, to the discerning eye, bearing my child, I did feel a surge of triumph because I'd pinned you down at last.'

She gasped.

'There's more,' he said gravely as he watched her shocked expression. He was still massaging her neck and they were very close. She could see the faint blue shadows on his jaw and, once again, that electrifying glint in his grey eyes.

'What?' she asked faintly.

'I've practised a certain kind of abstinence for nearly two months now, my dear. I'm like a man dying of hunger and thirst because, apart from one occasion, you haven't crooked a finger at me.'

Her eyes were suddenly huge. 'You didn't either.'

'Because I wasn't sure whether you wanted me, whether you were still concerned with that crazy notion of impropriety, whether you'd decided we should abstain until after the wedding. And all the time I've been missing out on everything that's been happening to you.'

'I...no, it wasn't anything like that, not really.'

He raised a wry eyebrow. 'Not really what, Clare?'

'I was afraid...' She hesitated. 'You said to me once that I was a joy to you as I was. But I'm not like that any longer, I may never be again—'

'Clare—are you serious?' He stared at her incredulously.

She clasped her hands. 'You don't know what it's like.'

'But surely you're not ashamed of—changing?'

'No,' she said intensely. 'But men—'

'You may not know as much about men as you think, Clare,' he interrupted.

'I know quite a bit about men as it happens,' she said with a slight challenge in her voice.

He smiled briefly. 'If you're talking about all the seamier side of them you've read about in your law books, perhaps. But I am in fact dying to not only see but touch this new you.'

She stared at him.

'That's why I brought you up here, as far away from home as I could think of, so we could be intensely private and intimate, and get back to the thing that matters most—you and I.'

She closed her eyes. 'I can't take issue with that, Lachlan.' And she leant against him with a little sigh of pleasure. 'But I must warn you I have changed.'

'How was that?' he said some time later.

They were lying on the vast bed in each other's arms.

'That was very decorous and—appropriate,' she said gravely. 'Especially for someone as starved as you.'

He propped his head on his hand and traced the new, more generous curves of her body. 'Are you complaining?'

'Well, you know how I like my sex. A little adventurous—'

'And with strange men,' he contributed with a wicked smile curving his mouth. 'But I thought we'd decided, or you'd decided, to be proper and matronly.'

'Matronly?' She sat up suddenly. 'I don't know why but the last thing I feel at the moment is matronly, and I was teasing you.' She glinted her own little wicked look down at him. 'That was *lovely*. And it brought home to me just what I'd been missing out on these last two months.'

'Clare—' he drew her back down beside him '—you know, you always surprise me.' But he was laughing.

'Do I? Tell me.' She settled herself comfortably with her head pillowed on his shoulder and curled the springy hairs on his chest through her fingers.

'Well,' he said, 'when I first met you, I was intrigued. You were so cool and brainy but the more I watched you, and then later thought about you, I couldn't help wondering what you'd be like in bed.'

'Talk about a typical man,' she reproved.

'And it grew until I knew that I had to find out— would you be cool and brainy in bed? Or—'

'Lachlan!'

'But you surprised me. You were tantalizing, fascinating, and I used to have these fantasies—that beneath that elegant, classy but definitely cool exterior there lurked a wild and wonderful lover and I was the only one who could turn it on.'

She started to protest but thought better of it. 'You're right,' she said. 'What happens to me with you never happened before and I never thought it would.'

'But then,' he said significantly, 'there were still times when you would go away from me, into your own little world of work, and you'd look at me as if I were a complete stranger—'

'I didn't—did I?'

'I remember a couple of occasions when I came to see you at work, and you were distant and reserved. I had an awful compulsion to lock the door and have my way with you on your beautiful oak desk, or the floor.'

She lifted her head and stared into his eyes, bemused. 'I didn't know,' she whispered.

'And that's the other thing that surprises me about

you, Clare. You often don't have the slightest idea of what you do to me.'

'You...don't you mind?'

'Yes and no. When I can bring you back to me like this—' he touched first one nipple then the other and she trembled and leant her forehead against his chest '—not at all. As for being decorous and appropriate,' he went on, 'we do need to consider Tweedledum and Tweedledee.'

She caught her breath on a gurgle of laughter. 'I know. I'm still dazed about that.'

He put his hand on the curve of her belly. 'There are many ways. Let me show you another.' And he pulled the pillows up behind him and sat her astride him.

Clare caught her breath again as she rested on her hands on the hard wall of his chest. Then, as he watched her intently, she straightened and he took in every movement of her fuller breasts, the curves of her shoulders and the mound of her belly.

Something possessed her—perhaps the admiration in his eyes—and she stretched her arms upwards. He pulled his knees up and she leant back against them and gasped as he cupped her breasts and teased her nipples with his thumbs.

Then he said barely audibly, 'Don't move.'

'Why not? It's...too nice,' she said huskily.

'Because if you do it will be—all over for me.'

'Ah. On the other hand, would it matter if I had the same problem?' Her aquamarine eyes were perfectly serious.

He took an unsteady breath and wondered if she had any idea how her new rich and generous curves suited her. How the midnight gloss of her tangled curls complemented the pale sheen of her skin and the ripening and darkening of her nipples, together with their heightened sensitivity, tantalized him almost unbearably.

Then she did move and they were swept away on a tide of splendid pleasure.

'Less decorous and appropriate?' he murmured into her hair a while later.

'Mmm,' she responded.

'What are you thinking about?' he asked as they lay in a voluptuous tangle of limbs, dewed with perspiration and palpably sated.

'Not shoes or ships and sealing wax,' she said dreamily. 'Not cabbages—definitely kings.'

'Clare—' he held her close '—that's what you do to me. I hope you believe it now.'

'I do,' she said quietly, and fell asleep in his arms. It was something she didn't take issue with even in the privacy of her mind for the rest of their honeymoon.

After breakfast the next morning they decided to go for a swim.

Clare eyed herself in her new maternity swimming costume and said, 'I see.'

He raised an eyebrow at her. 'What?'

'That this was a mistake.' She studied herself in the mirror in the pretty enough costume, primrose-yellow with little white polka dots, but it was obvious she didn't enjoy the view.

'What's wrong with it?' he asked with a frown.

She plucked at the frilled skirt that fell from below

the bust to the tops of her thighs and concealed an expanding panel beneath it. 'I'll tell you: it makes me feel tubby, matronly and about a hundred years old.'

'Now you mention it,' he murmured, 'your bikinis were better.'

'I can't fit into any of my bikinis and even if I could I'd feel a bit funny—all of which is your fault, Mr Hewitt!'

'You mean I did this to you?' he queried.

'Well—yes!'

'Then perhaps I can come up with a solution,' he said slowly. 'Stay there.' He walked out.

Clare, who wasn't feeling seriously aggrieved, sat down on the bed to wait.

He came back twenty minutes later and tipped the contents of a resort shop bag onto the bed. Two bikinis fell out with two T-shirts.

'But,' she said, 'I—'

'Hang on. They're a couple of sizes larger.' He picked up one pair, a lovely concoction of emerald Lycra, and picked up the soft jade T-shirt in his other hand. 'For public consumption you could wear the T-shirt over the top. It probably wouldn't hurt to wear a shirt while you swim anyway; the sun is pretty powerful up here. But for private consumption—that is to say, for my eyes only—you could leave the shirt off.'

Clare stared at him.

'Same goes for this combination,' he said, and discarded the emerald pair and shirt to lift up the other pair—wild rice Lycra this time with a matching

T-shirt. 'Of course, for private consumption, you could leave not only the shirt but the top off as well.'

Still Clare said nothing.

'You don't approve?'

'I...think you're a genius!' She jumped up and kissed him. 'Why didn't I think of that?' She started to strip off the offending maternity suit.

'You have a very serious turn of mind for the most part?' he suggested.

She chuckled. 'You're also a darling!'

'There's more.' But he waited until she was in the emerald bikini with the T-shirt on before he went outside and returned with two hats, a pair of fuchsia-pink canvas shoes and a straw tote bag.

'Lachlan! Is there anything left in the shop?'

'Plenty more. Now this hat—' he held up a glorious broad-brimmed raffia hat with a green and fuchsia silk scarf around the crown '—is for lazing and sunbathing. Whereas this one—' he picked up a sporty little peaked baseball cap '—is for when we're more active in the sun, boating et cetera. So are the shoes.'

Clare donned the big hat carefully, setting it straight on her head and fluffing out her hair beneath it at the back. She slipped the shoes on and slung the straw bag over her shoulder. The effect was immediately glamorous, the shirt all but disguised her pregnant state, and all of a sudden she felt like a million dollars in comparison to how she'd felt earlier.

'I can't believe it,' she said. 'I mean that you have such good taste in clothes, such a sense of colour as well as good taste in—' She stopped.

'In women?' he drawled. He had his shoulders propped against the door frame and he wore a pair of blue board shorts with a grey T-shirt. His feet were bare.

'I mean—I didn't mean…how did that come out?' she asked helplessly.

He shrugged. 'I have to agree about my taste in women,' he said lazily as he ran his grey eyes over her. He smiled slightly as she coloured a bit.

'But,' he added, 'I have to *confess*,' he paused and she waited, wide-eyed '…that the girl in the shop is responsible for choosing all this.' He waved a hand. 'She knew exactly what colours and styles would suit you. By the way, she also complimented me on my taste in women.'

'Even though I'm pregnant?' Clare looked surprised.

'That's what you don't seem to understand—how much it becomes you.'

Clare grimaced. 'Oh, well, I'll take your word for it.'

'No, that's not good enough—believe it, Clare. You're a sight for sore eyes. You're radiant—'

'And blooming, shortly to become what they call a visual overload!' She stopped laughing and said softly and warmly, 'I do believe it. How could I not? Thank you. For restoring my confidence and spending a small fortune in the process.' She kissed him again and said gaily, 'Shall we swim, Mr Hewitt?'

He didn't reply but took her hand and looked down into her eyes for a long moment in a way that was quizzical yet oddly enigmatic. Then he kissed her knuckles and murmured, 'After you, Mrs Hewitt.'

Clare blinked. 'That's the first time.'

He raised an eyebrow at her.

'Anyone's called me Mrs Hewitt.'

His lips twisted. 'How does it feel?'

'Very…grand,' she said slowly. 'It has a…solid, proper ring to it.'

'Much better than Ms Montrose, I agree.'

'I explained about that.'

'I know. That was our first little run-in, if I recall correctly.'

'As a matter of fact, you're wrong,' Clare said. 'My first run-in with you, although I may not have let on, was to do with the way you looked me up and down extremely thoroughly the first time you laid eyes on me.'

He laughed softly. 'I was surprised.'

'Why?' She looked mystified.

'I knew you had to be brainy but I also expected you to be… I don't think I ought to say it.'

'A dog?' she queried dangerously.

'I wouldn't have put it quite like that but—'

'How like a typical man!'

'That's the second time you've said that to me in two days.'

She stared at him with her lips compressed then they eased a bit and finally they curved into a smile. 'I must admit I was surprised, too. Even impressed, although against my better judgement.'

He laughed. 'There you go. But to get back to what brought this on—shall we swim, Mrs Hewitt?'

'Yes, please, Mr Hewitt,' she said humorously.

*   *   *

They spent their days swimming, lying on the beach, fishing and sailing. They took an excursion to Zoe Bay in a hired motor cruiser.

On the eastern side of Hinchinbrook, Zoe Bay had beaches and walks, one up a rock-strewn creek bed to a rock pool below a waterfall. They swam beneath the waterfall then climbed down and swam again from a beach up the north arm of the bay. There was absolutely no one in sight of this beach, so they swam without their clothes in the green-tinted clear water and the high craggy peaks of Hinchinbrook floated in the blue sky above them.

Clare's skin began to look like pale honey and she glowed with health. Lachlan made her take a rest every afternoon although he himself often went scuba-diving or water-skiing, both pursuits not recommended for pregnant ladies.

And she would often awake from her afternoon nap to find him leaning over her and teasing her eyebrow with the tip of his finger or kissing her toes.

It was very hot and the short dusks of the tropics came as a welcome relief. And after they'd watched the sun set she would retire to their room, leaving him to chat to other guests, and get ready for dinner.

It was on their fourth night that it happened. She'd washed her hair, showered the mixture of salt and sand off her body, smoothed moisturizer all over her and debated what to wear while she dried and styled her hair. In the end she chose a long almond-coloured dress, with a scooped neck, cap sleeves and gathered below her breasts. A row of tiny gold buttons ran down the front and she slipped on gold sandals and her pearls.

Then she reached for a creamy hibiscus from the flower arrangement and lifted her arms to pin it into her hair, but stopped.

Lachlan came in at that point and took in her raised arms, her wide eyes and her frozen stance. 'What's wrong?' he said immediately.

'I…nothing…I don't know.' She lowered her arms and put her hands on her stomach. 'It moved, I think,' she said in an awed voice. 'I mean they moved, or one of them did. How incredible!'

He came across and put his hands on her stomach. But after a moment he kissed the tip of her nose and said he could feel nothing.

'Well, it was just a feather touch but I'm sure it was that— There it goes again!'

'I'm sure you're right.'

'There, there, baby—*babies*,' she crooned to her stomach. 'Mama's here!'

He laughed as he pulled off his shirt. 'We'll have to start thinking about names. Any preferences?' he called from the shower.

'Definitely not Tweedledum and Tweedledee! And I don't know what they are, which makes it difficult. I could have known if I'd wanted to but I decided to be traditional— No, that's not correct,' she amended. 'I just couldn't think straight.'

He came out of the shower wrapped in a towel. 'Then we'd better have two sets of boys' names and two sets of girls' names ready,' he said wryly. 'Personally, I've always liked Tom.' He threw his towel away and started to dress.

Clare sat down on the bed and watched him. She always enjoyed the ritual of watching him dress, not only because he was a joy to behold in all the lean, muscled glory of his body but because he did it with such decision. No humming and ha-ing for this member of the male species, she thought with secret amusement, but she wondered what would happen if it wasn't all there, clean and pressed and where it should be for him.

Not that she had had anything to do with it—Orpheus took great care of its guests in every respect. But she realized she would have much to do with it when they got home, and she blinked several times.

'Clare?' He stood before her, tucking a crisp white T-shirt into navy cotton trousers. 'Don't you like Tom? It is your father's—'

'I know and I do like it and he's already asked for it. So that's one settled but I was thinking of something else.'

He sat down beside her. 'Oh?'

'Yes, how you would be if I'm not the best housekeeper in the world,' she said gravely.

'Ah! I thought you might have guessed.'

'Not—really,' she said with a slight frown at his unusually stern expression.

'An absolute ogre—if my meals aren't to my liking and my shirts aren't ironed properly I'm liable to cut all your privileges, beat you black and blue—'

'No, seriously,' she said laughingly.

'Seriously?' He eyed her perfectly seriously. 'Move to a hotel? No, I don't give a damn to be honest—what brought this on?'

'I was watching the way you dress.'

'Clare—' he took her hand '—it wouldn't take much of that kind of talk to make me undress.'

'No—'

'No? Don't tell me, you're starving,' he said mournfully.

'Well, I am,' she conceded, 'but don't you forget I'm eating for three. Not that you should think that way, I've read, but, well—how did we get onto this?'

'You said no, very definitely no.' He looked hurt but there was a wicked glint in his eyes that she knew well.

'I wasn't talking about that at all, as it happens.'

'It goes from bad to worse—you were watching me dress with quite other thoughts on your mind? Are you tired of me already, Clare?'

'Lachlan, will you just shut up?' she warned although her eyes were dancing.

'Be my guest,' he invited.

'I was watching the way you dress and it struck me that you do it with all the confidence of a man who is supremely used to having everything in its rightful place—as if you've never in your life had to search for matching socks or clean shirts.'

'Clare—' he stared at her '—are you serious?'

'Yes. Yes, I am.' She shrugged at his look of bemusement. 'I can't help it, that's what was going through my mind, which led me to wonder how successful I would be—at that kind of thing.'

'Bloody hell—I just do it, I've never even thought about it—'

'As I suspected,' she said gravely.

'Is this seriously going to interfere with our love life?'

'No...'

'I think I need more reassurance. Otherwise I'll be

plagued by the thought that every time you see me without my clothes the laundering and sorting and hanging up of them will leap into your mind and—'

'Will you stop being such an idiot?' she said through her laughter and leant her cheek on his shoulder.

'So the answer's still no?' He kissed the top of her head.

'Yes! Well, until after dinner at least.'

'That's better,' he said slowly, 'but I think I ought to take out a little insurance—any idea what I have in mind?'

'Yes, this,' she said promptly, and wound her arms around his neck and kissed him passionately.

For some reason this sobered him genuinely, and he looked down at her for a long moment, his eyes unreadable.

'What now?' she asked softly.

At last a touch of humour lit his eyes and twisted his lips. 'If it took an army of housekeepers to preserve this kind of status quo between us, Clare, I'd do it.'

'Oh, I think one might be enough—shall we go and eat?'

The rest of their honeymoon sped by.

On their last night they sat on the veranda steps outside their room holding hands and she said, 'Thank you for a lovely honeymoon. It's going to be hard to leave all this.'

'I'm glad to hear you say that.'

She raised an eyebrow at him.

'I thought you might be champing at the bit to get back to work.'

'Lachlan, did I look as if I was?'

He studied her hand, turning her plain gold wedding ring round and round with his fingers. She had a pink Argyle diamond engagement ring that matched the stone on her pearls to go with it but wasn't wearing it. 'No,' he said at last, 'but I don't always know what you're thinking.'

She smiled ruefully. 'Nine times out of ten you seem to.'

'So you're not in a fever to get back to work?'

'No, I'm not. For once in my life, no.'

'Do you think that will change when we do get back?'

'I...' She paused.

'Or,' he said slowly, 'is it a bit like stepping off the end of the earth—going back tomorrow?'

She took a breath and realized suddenly that it was. That subconsciously she had blocked it from her mind—not hard to do with the perfection of their honeymoon but all the same... 'A little,' she confessed. 'I haven't been able to think about it, or wanted to, I guess. But I'm sure I'll be fine. Let's not spoil our last night, it's been so perfect—'

'Clare, I'm in complete agreement about not spoiling our last night and *you've* been perfect, but I think it's better to talk about it now,' he said firmly. 'Otherwise this could become a separate zone with an unreal quality to it. But it shouldn't *be* possible to spoil it simply by talking about the rest of our lives.'

She bit her lip as she saw the truth of his words. 'I didn't really mean that.' She stopped and sighed.

'But I have to say that after we decided to get married and I went back to Rosemont I couldn't—I just couldn't picture myself there.'

She flinched inwardly as soon as she'd said it and waited for his reaction a bit nervously.

But he surprised her. 'That's only to be expected. I think most married couples expect to start out in a place of their own, but if not that certainly not the domain of a previous wife.'

Clare glanced at him, taken aback.

He met her glance squarely. 'We're also going to encounter plenty of times when we have to talk about Serena, and I don't want it to hurt or upset you when we do.'

She looked out into the night for a long moment. 'I think I understand what you're trying to do, Lachlan. Build a bridge between this—magic—and ordinary everyday life.'

He released her hand but put his arm around her shoulders. 'I always knew you were brainy. And it's not a bad idea to take it with us, is it?'

She laid her cheek against his chest. 'For the difficult times?' she said slowly.

'Do you think I didn't see you walking through Rosemont as if it were an alien planet? Do you think I haven't noticed you walking through the macadamias and avocados, looking over your shoulder as if you're expecting some ghost to jump out at you? It's one of—' He stopped abruptly.

'Go on.'

'So I do know there are times when it won't be easy for you, Clare. But there's no reason why we can't take this magic with us.'

'No.' She said it almost absently.

'You don't sound too sure.'

'Will you mind if I do go back to work, though?'

'Part-time, not at all. I think it would be good for you. As long as you don't over-tire yourself,' he said wryly.

Of course this was eminently sensible, she agreed inwardly, and was probably a decision she would have made herself, but she felt a little niggle of unease. Because he had made it?

But that was supremely negative thinking, she warned herself. No way to start this marriage of—what? she wondered suddenly. Not only convenience on her part because if she'd thought she was deeply in love with him before she now knew it had grown in the past week to almost unmanageable proportions. To the extent of barely being able to stop herself from telling him.

But, although they'd made love and had all the appearance of being in love, the words 'I love you' had remained unsaid by either of them.

Perhaps she had to prove herself as a wife before he'd say it, she pondered. Was that what this 'bridge' was all about? And she had the sudden chill little conviction that she might have hit the nail on the head.

Then she felt it. Not such a feather feeling this time but a little tap then a series of little taps. She put her hands on her stomach and could feel the movement through her fingers. And it was as if her whole being was turned inwards suddenly, to the life within her, the two lives, an almost mystical moment that reduced everything else to mere pinpricks.

She turned her face to Lachlan and it was calm and serene. 'I'll be fine,' she said quietly.

CHAPTER SIX

THEY flew home the next morning.

Lachlan had left the Range Rover in the security car park at Brisbane Airport. It was a three-hour drive to Rosemont from Brisbane but they stopped for lunch at Byron Bay then made another stop at Clare's office in Lennox Head at Lachlan's suggestion.

Sue was working although it was a Saturday afternoon and she welcomed Clare with open arms and many comments on how marvellously well she looked.

'Thanks for that,' she said to Lachlan as they drove towards Rosemont at last. 'She seems to have everything pretty much under control,' she added wryly.

'Feeling relegated?' he asked with a touch of humour.

'A little,' she confessed.

'I would take it as a compliment to what a well-oiled machine you had up and running in the first place,' he suggested.

'You're too nice. Talking of relegated, I guess you're dying to see how many nuts have fallen?' she said mischievously.

'I...would never be able to relegate you, Clare, but, in a word, yes.'

119

'You have my blessing,' she said serenely. 'I've got to unpack and—' She gestured. 'Plenty to do.'

He glanced at her with something unfathomable in his eyes then it was replaced by a glint of devilry. 'You don't have to attack the laundry, Clare.'

'Well, I may and I may not, Lachlan.' They turned up the drive and suddenly Paddy and Flynn were racing alongside the car. 'No Nez Percé,' she said ruefully.

'No.' He frowned faintly and drew up in the gravel square in front of the homestead. There was another car parked in the square, a shiny silver Mercedes convertible that Clare didn't recognize and neither did he, apparently, as his frown deepened. Then he swore as two people came out onto the veranda.

Clare blinked and her eyes widened. 'Not...?'

'Precisely. Serena and her new boyfriend.'

'Did you...last night...did you know?' she asked shakenly.

'No, of course not,' he said grimly, and got out. By this time May had emerged from the house, looking distinctly troubled. But Lachlan came round and helped Clare down the high step first, then took her hand and led her up the veranda stairs.

'Well, Serena,' he said, 'to what do we owe this visitation?'

Serena took her time. She examined Clare from head to toe and in the tense little pause Clare was able to form her own impressions, the chief one being that Serena was still dazzlingly beautiful. Her fair hair was sleek and shining, her cornflower-blue eyes large and expressive with a heavy fringe of lashes, her figure in jeans and a blue silk shirt stunning.

Then she flicked those cornflower eyes from Clare to Lachlan and she said in an attractively husky voice, 'You didn't waste much time, did you, Lachlan? I hope you warned your new wife that she's due to become a baby factory—'

'Serena.' Lachlan said it coolly and with obvious distaste. 'Just get on with it.'

But that only made her smile. 'Why are we here? We were in the district on holiday so I thought I'd pick up Sean and take him away with us for a few days. Only, there appears to be a problem. Now, I wonder how the Family Court would view it?' she said meditatively. 'Perhaps your new wife could enlighten us?'

'What problem?' This time Lachlan's voice was as hard as steel.

'The extent to which you've alienated Sean from me, Lachlan.' Serena's voice hardened, too. 'Even going to the length of impregnating your solicitor so you could marry her to be able to keep Sean here. I think they might have a problem with it,' she finished gently.

'I've done nothing to alienate Sean from you, he's always wanted to stay here and you've always been happy to have him out of your hair—'

'Tell him, May,' Serena interrupted.

May sighed heavily. 'He's locked himself in his room and gone on a hunger strike—rather than go with Serena.'

Sean abandoned his hunger strike, only an hour or so old as it happened, and unlocked his door as soon as he heard his father's voice.

He also said to his mother, 'Serena, don't take this personally but I want to live *here*. I'll come and see you often, though. Hey! I'll always be your kid and you'll always be my mum.'

Clare flinched from the flash of fury she saw in Serena's eyes, but the other woman, to give her credit, laughed suddenly and hugged him.

In all this, Serena's boyfriend was a somewhat bemused and silent spectator. Then he held out his hand to Lachlan and introduced himself as Bruce Davidson.

He was not as tall as Lachlan, balding, with a stocky build, but with plenty of evidence of his wealth displayed upon his person. A gold chain around his neck, a gold watch that must have cost thousands on his wrist; Gucci loafers worn with lime-green linen trousers and a bottle-green silk shirt that shouted either Armani or Versace; a gold and diamond studded key ring that he jiggled frequently.

But despite the clear contrast between these two men Clare found herself liking Bruce. Although she couldn't deny that the contrast between Lachlan's physique and sheer masculinity in his khaki moleskin trousers and checked shirt, and Bruce's colourful splendour, gave her an unholy moment of triumph over Serena Hewitt.

It was a tribute to May's diplomacy how this happened. She produced afternoon tea and insisted they all sit down to it.

At first Serena was silent and mutinous. But Bruce exerted himself to talk to both Clare and Lachlan, and, finding herself outgunned, perhaps, she gradually thawed, although there was something oddly chilling in the way her gaze rested on Clare now and then.

As for Clare herself, she felt a bit as if she were Alice at the Mad Hatter's tea party, but she responded to Bruce's olive branch and that was when she discovered he was rather nice. Shrewd, probably, she divined, down-to-earth and possessed of a keen sense of humour, and not unkind. She judged him to be a few years older than Lachlan.

It also became clear to her that Serena would not always get her own way with this man, despite his obvious devotion to her. He told them openly that this was his first bite of the cherry, his first marriage, and he was looking forward to the day when they had children of their own.

'I'll have half-brothers and sisters popping out all over,' Sean commented ruefully, and got a cool look from his father.

'You know,' Bruce said thoughtfully and softly to Clare, 'I misjudged that kid. Serena told me he was very bright, but how bloody bright can an eight-year-old be, I said to myself? He's only a kid!'

'This one—extremely,' she said wryly.

'So maybe I talked down to him and frightened him off?'

'Uh—maybe.'

Bruce jiggled his key ring. 'I'll give it some thought. I hear you're expecting twins?'

'Yes. And beginning to look and feel like it,' she said.

His gaze travelled unembarrassedly over her. She was wearing her yellow-and-white overblouse and white leggings. Then he said, 'I think you look marvellous!'

Unfortunately these words fell into a little pause in the conversation from the rest of the table, and Serena shot Clare the deadliest look before swiftly veiling her eyes—leaving Clare with the clear understanding that Lachlan's first wife hated her thoroughly without even knowing her.

If this wasn't enough, as they were leaving, Bruce turned to look at the old homestead surrounded by its rose gardens and said, 'Got a lot of class, this place. I might borrow some ideas from it.'

'If it wasn't so serious it would have been funny,' Clare said, later that evening. 'Sean's amazingly resourceful if nothing else.'

'I suppose it had its moments,' Lachlan said.

They were sitting in the den. Sean was in bed asleep and May had retired to her own area of the house, a separate wing.

'Bruce wasn't exactly tactful, either,' Lachlan added with a glint of humour.

'I liked him,' Clare said slowly. 'Whereas Serena is obviously not going to like me whatever I do.'

'She may have bitten off more than she can chew, in answer to your first observation, Clare. But I wouldn't worry about whether she likes you or not. It's not common for first wives to like their replacements.'

Especially if they resent being replaced and still love or want their first husbands, Clare mused inwardly.

'By the way, I don't expect you to be a baby factory,' he said.

Clare glanced at him. He was sitting on a low ottoman beside her chair with his hands around one knee and, because he was lower than she was, she was in the unusual position of being able to see the top of his head, although not, at that moment, his eyes.

'Quite unwittingly and not your fault on this occasion, I may feel like one from time to time,' she said humorously. 'But was that one of the reasons you got divorced? Because she wouldn't have any more children?'

He didn't answer for a while and when he did it was still only the top of his head she could see. 'Yes,' he said finally. 'I did want more. I thought it would be good for Sean, and I thought it might reduce her preoccupation with herself. And I probably suffer from an only-child syndrome—did you ever, Clare?' He looked up at her at last.

It took her by surprise and only later occurred to her that he was changing the subject. 'As a matter of fact, I used to long for brothers and sisters when I was growing up. I can remember thinking that it...' she paused and narrowed her eyes '...gave one a built-in advantage when it came to interacting with other kids.'

He nodded his agreement.

'Of course I now know,' she went on, 'that big families are renowned for feuds and all sorts of jealousies not to mention the lack of attention the children lower down the order suffer from.'

'Through sheer weight of exhaustion on the part

of their parents,' he contributed. 'Perhaps we were luckier than we knew. Talking of it, you look tired.'

'I...' she suddenly yawned uncontrollably '...I'm exhausted all of a sudden.'

He stood up. 'Bed, then, Mrs Hewitt.' He held his hand down to her and helped her up. 'By the way, you were brilliant throughout that whole unseemly shemozzle.'

She hesitated then said only, 'Thanks!'

'This is lovely.' She looked around the large bedroom that he'd told her would be theirs, but with an odd little inflection in her voice.

It had a pressed iron high ceiling painted white, creamy yellow walls and yellow and pink floral curtains and bedspread. There was a fireplace and two comfortable armchairs in front of it covered in pink velvet. The furniture was all old, lovely cedar pieces with brass fittings and the bed was vast.

Their bags, still unpacked, stood on the floor in the middle of the room.

Lachlan drew the curtains. 'It was the official guest bedroom,' he said. 'But seeing that it's the nicest bedroom with the best views I decided it should be ours.'

Clare digested this and realized it was his way of telling her that he and Serena had never used it. At the same time it struck her as a little strange that only last night he was the one who had been concerned about her being hurt or upset by any mention of Serena. Yet, if anything, he was now the one who was balking at any direct mention of his ex-wife.

She sat down on the end of the bed feeling help-

less, but without the will or the strength to sort
through all the implications, let alone all the innu-
endoes the extraordinary day had produced.

Lachlan studied her for a moment then opened her
bag and drew out a nightgown as well as her toilet
bag. He handed her the toilet bag and said gently,
'Clean your teeth and wash your face. The bathroom's through there.'

She didn't argue and came back presently.

He helped her to undress, sliding the white cotton,
pin-tucked nightgown over her head and kissing the
tip of her nose as it emerged. Then he turned down
the cover and invited her to slip into the bed.

She hesitated. 'Are you coming?'

'Shortly. I don't think I could sleep yet and there
are a few things I could do but I'll only be in my
study.'

She got into bed and lay there with her hair spread
out on the pillow like dark, rough silk on the crisp
yellow pillowcase, and couldn't resist a little sigh of
pleasure. The bed was wonderfully comfortable.

'Close your eyes,' he said softly.

She did so.

'Sweet dreams, Mrs Hewitt. I'm right here in the
house if you need me.' He kissed her eyelids, then
the light went off and she was alone.

She turned on her side, slipped her hand under her
cheek and wondered why she was so composed. Because she had no doubt there were dark waters lapping between Lachlan and Serena, and something
oddly unfinished. Yet it seemed not to touch her directly.

She couldn't feel the same hatred Serena so obviously did; there was no bubble of hysteria at the thought that Lachlan might never rid himself of a dangerous attraction to a woman he also despised, or claimed he did. No sheer panic to think that Sean *had* been the reason for their marriage.

She curved her hand protectively around her stomach, and felt a series of little taps.

That's it, she thought with sudden comprehension as a feeling of wonder flooded her again. She was curiously insulated from it all because of the two lives growing within her.

She fell asleep and didn't stir when Lachlan slid in beside her, didn't stir until sunlight glowed through the curtains.

'I don't want to rush into things,' May said the next morning, a Sunday, 'but now you're the lady of the house perhaps we should discuss them.'

They were sharing a pot of fragrant coffee after breakfast. Lachlan and Sean had just left them to do an inspection of the estate.

'So if you'd rather have the place to yourself, Clare, you only need to tell me,' May continued seriously. 'I would quite understand.'

'May,' Clare said, 'I don't know what arrangement you had with Serena but I'd very much appreciate your staying put! Not only because I like you and know this is more your home than mine—'

'Clare, it isn't really,' May said with a troubled expression. 'I own shares in the family company that runs the estate but Lachlan is the main shareholder and he directly inherited the house and property, so…'

She paused as if she didn't quite know how to go on, then said, 'But although Serena found it convenient to have me run the house while she took most of the glory for it, as well as help with Sean, I very much regret falling into that trap.'

Clare looked at her wide-eyed.

'I often wonder whether it mightn't have turned out better if they'd been left to themselves,' May said, then flinched. 'I...I...'

'It's all right,' Clare said quietly. 'You don't have to worry about guarding your tongue all the time. I'm not going to be super-sensitive and silly. But if you're trying to say that Lachlan and I might be better on our own I can't answer you yet.'

'I would never forgive myself if it happened again and I had any part in it,' May said. 'But then I keep thinking, with twins on the way...' She stopped and sighed.

'Would it take a whole burden off your shoulders if I said perhaps you're right and we do need to be on our own?' Clare said slowly.

This time May heaved a sigh of relief but murmured anxiously, 'Are you sure you understand, Clare? I would come back if ever you needed me, I'd definitely come back for a time to help with the babies—'

'May, you will always be a part of Rosemont to my mind, always.'

May blinked and blew her nose. 'Thanks. The other thing is, I'm only sixty-five—' she grimaced '—but I've always longed to travel. Well, I *have*, but there's always been a time limit whereas now I could

really indulge one of my pet passions—archae-
ology—'

'Do it, May,' Clare said. 'Just give me a week.
Running a household can't be much different from
running a law practice, surely?'

'You're a darling,' May said with warmth and
tears in her eyes again. 'And don't you let Serena
bother you. She may be the sexiest thing since
Cleopatra but I couldn't help secretly cheering when
Lachlan did divorce her.'

May broke her news over lunch and it was plain to
see that she'd taken Lachlan supremely by surprise.

'I'm sure you don't have to,' he said slowly, and
frowned.

'I have Clare's blessing,' May murmured.

'Definitely. You were the one who complimented
me only yesterday on what an up-and-running, well-
oiled machine I'd produced,' Clare said to him with
dancing eyes.

'I know but that was work—'

'Oh, after a week with May, I'm sure I can trans-
late it to—what do they call it so tweely?—home
duties, that's it.'

He seemed about to say something, then, as Sean
looked interested, changed his mind. And he asked
May about her plans instead.

It wasn't until that evening that he got the chance
to ask Clare to elaborate.

She was sitting at the dressing table brushing her
hair prior to going to bed, but she turned on the stool
and told him simply why May wanted to go.

'I see,' he said abruptly. Then, 'I don't see how

you're going to cope and I'm not sure if she *really* wants to go.'

'Lachlan...'

She paused and studied him as he stood with an arm resting on the fireplace mantel. He hadn't changed although she had her nightgown on with a grey satin robe over it, and she knew instinctively she would be going to bed by herself again. She also knew instinctively that he was not in a good mood and that she was the chief reason for it, although she had so rarely seen him other than even-tempered.

The pressures of married life? she wondered, and raised an eyebrow.

'What?' he said coolly.

'I think you should credit me with some sense, Lachlan,' she said equally coolly.

'Well, I think *you* should remember that you're nearly five months pregnant, with twins, you want to keep on working and there's Sean to be taken into consideration.'

'All right, let's take it point by point in reverse order,' she answered crisply. 'The biggest factor in Sean's life is you. Now, it may be a little wrench for him to lose May but he's made a very positive statement to the effect that he can abide me if nothing else so long as he still has the central pivot of Rosemont and *you*.'

'Clare—'

'No, let me finish. And if I can—and I will—tread slowly and carefully so that he feels safe, valued and listened to rather than smothered with false affection, if he's never made to feel that I've come between you, he should be fine.'

'That may sound all very well in theory, Clare, in fact that's how it does sound—straight out of some textbook on how to handle stepchildren. It may not always work that way.'

'Ah, but you're assuming I resent Sean or he resents me,' she shot back.

'Sometimes one isn't aware of these things.'

'I *know* I don't resent Sean and he will have no reason to resent me. The next point is twins and being five months pregnant. None of that is going to interfere with my mental processes, none of it is going to reduce me to an invalid in the normal course of events. OK, as you took pains to tell me, I might be slow and heavy for a while, but I can get help, it's as simple as that.'

'You missed one of my key points, Clare. Work. Not that many weeks ago you were telling me you were so career-orientated, you were sure you'd be better off as a single parent.'

She gasped; she couldn't believe he could throw that up at her. So much so, she threw her brush down and stood up with her eyes glinting fire. 'You bastard,' she said softly. 'I'll tell you what happened. I made my bed and now I'm going to lie in it. And I'm going to do it as well as I can and I don't need May to feel press-ganged into being my crutch!'

They stared at each other until she added, 'Please feel free to go and do some work but I'm going to bed.'

Still he said nothing, then he straightened and simply walked out.

This time she was still awake when he came to bed, not that much later.

And he pulled her into his arms despite her convulsive stiffening and murmur of protest. 'Don't,' he breathed against her hair. 'I'm sorry. It's such a load for you to take on and I know you were worried about it, I guess that's why I got a shock about May.'

She relaxed slightly but said nothing.

'Could you see your way clear to humouring me a little, Clare?'

'Humouring you—what do you mean?'

He reached out and switched one bedside lamp on then stared down at her with his head propped on his hand. 'Still angry, still so beautiful,' he said quietly as he ran his hand through her hair then cupped her cheek. 'Look, Serena set me off base yesterday and now this. I'm sorry but I'd have given anything for you not to have had her particular brand of bitchiness and venom directed squarely at you.'

'Serena,' Clare said, and hesitated, 'used to—the thought of her used to upset me. She has absolutely no power over me now, Lachlan.'

He moved his fingers on her cheek and seemed about to say something then to change his mind. 'How are they?'

'Who?'

'Tweedledum and Tweedledee?'

'They're fine. Resting, I believe.'

'Good. My apologies to them, too. For making you as mad as fire.'

A rueful smile curved Clare's lips. 'I don't honestly think they noticed. You know, I read this incredible survey once, about babies conceived in close proximity to Tokyo Airport. Their mothers lived with the continual noise of jet aircraft flying low overhead.'

'It didn't upset them in the womb?'

'Apparently not because once they were born they were much happier back amongst the jets.'

'Does that mean—what does that mean?' he asked with a grin.

'I'm not sure, it just occurred to me. But perhaps that you don't need to worry too much about external things affecting them. Although I wouldn't like to be unhappy too often.'

'In case you pass on the vibes. Are you unhappy right now, Clare? Have I made you unhappy?'

'I wasn't feeling a million quid,' she conceded.

'You were also extremely concise and lawyerly— until you mentioned a bed, that is.'

She looked into his eyes then grimaced. 'That wasn't my best legalese.'

He bent his head and kissed her on the lips. 'What I'm wondering now, though—and that's why I asked if you could humour me—is whether the fact that the bed in question happens also to be *my* bed has anything going for it at all?'

'It was a figure of speech at the time—'

'The way you said it seemed to indicate that it didn't have anything going for it. Was it just a slip of the tongue in the heat of the moment?'

Clare moved, but not to draw away. 'To be honest,' she said thoughtfully, 'at the time, the last thing I wanted to do was share your bed, Lachlan.'

'How about now?'

'If— Do you really want it?' She bit her lip.

Something flickered in his eyes. 'Let me show you,' he murmured, however.

And he started to make exquisitely tender love to her.

'You've won me over,' she whispered at one stage.

'I think it's the opposite, you've won this round game, set and match,' he said unevenly, and buried his head between her breasts.

She was awake when he woke the next morning, lying quietly on her side watching him as the curtains filtered the sunlight.

He slept mostly on his back and she saw his eyes open, then he stretched luxuriously and turned to her. 'Mmm...' he murmured, and took her in his arms. 'What have I done to deserve this?' He nuzzled her neck and stroked her back.

'Deserve what?'

'To have a naked, extremely desirable, soft, warm, pliant and gorgeous creature like you in my bed.'

'I'm only naked because I fell asleep that way.' She looked at him severely. 'After you'd had your way with me— Don't,' she said on a little gasp as he plucked her nipple gently between his teeth.

'Sorry—sore?' he queried, looking into her eyes.

'I...not really, just...' She stopped and wondered how to explain that it was almost too much pleasure he was inflicting on her.

But he said, 'Never mind, I shall desist, but only because I have to be up, dressed and fed in approximately two minutes and twelve seconds.'

'How can you know that?'

'Are you saying you don't want me to desist?' he enquired with little points of laughter in the smoky grey of his eyes.

'No. I mean…what I was *thinking* was that you hadn't even looked at your watch!'

'I know exactly what the time is due to the quality of the sunlight,' he said seriously. 'However, if that was not the only thought on your mind, my foreman, who I had arranged to meet in one minute and fifty-seven seconds now, could quite easily start without me.'

'I don't know about that. I think you should set a good example of punctuality towards your staff otherwise they may be tempted to copy your slack ways.'

'Are you lecturing me, Clare?'

'Definitely—not. I wouldn't dream of it,' she replied demurely.

'All the same you are. Unless you just don't feel like letting me have my way with you again? Because you haven't entirely forgiven me?'

Clare took a little breath then smiled suddenly. 'I hadn't entirely forgiven you last night, yet—look what happened to me.'

'Didn't you enjoy it?'

'I…loved every minute of it, as you very well know, but I wasn't really expecting to.' Her gaze softened and she reached out to touch his hair.

'Then I think we could afford a repeat performance. I'd be useless anyway with the thought of it on my mind—' He stopped as the phone on the bedside table rang, and swore.

When he put it down, Clare was laughing.

'See—you didn't believe me, did you?' he said wryly.

'No, I didn't. He wants to know if he should start without you, I gather?'

'Well, he would have but he can't get the picker started. Still—'

It was a light tap on the door this time that interrupted him. And Sean's voice imparting the news that his football required blowing up, it was the first day of footy practice at school therefore most important that his ball was operational, and had they forgotten it was a school day anyway?

'I'm coming,' Lachlan called resignedly. 'Bloody hell,' he added, and hugged Clare. 'I'm jinxed, destined to have a thoroughly uncomfortable day and all you can do is laugh!'

'I know, and you're very sweet,' Clare said, still laughing.

'Sweet?' He raised a pained eyebrow at her.

'Yes,' she insisted, and kissed him. 'Go and sort everything out. I make no promises but if you are dreadfully uncomfortable, well, you've got me into the habit of having a nap after lunch, which is *before* school comes out and when the rest of the world generally takes a break. So.'

'I never realized that one day I would treasure a simple little word and carry it with me like a beacon through the morning. So...' he said lingeringly. 'A name I'd never have thought of for it.'

'Do you always wake up as playful as this?'

'Only when I'm not sure of my welcome,' he said ruefully, and made no move to get up.

Clare sighed theatrically. 'You're forgiven.'

'I knew I could make you say it.' His eyes teased her, but before she could take issue he did get up. 'Stay there, I'll bring you some tea and toast. You'll find,' he said over his shoulder just before he disappeared into the shower, 'that you won't have any complaints about how caring a husband I am, as well as, of course, sexy.'

Clare drank her tea and ate her toast and marmalade in a somewhat bemused state. Because she couldn't identify what had made him change so completely from the cold and annoyed man of the night before.

Was it something she'd done? Or hadn't done, she mused. He hadn't appeared to like any of her arguments at the time.

But nothing presented itself and presently she got up and got dressed.

She only went into work a couple of times in the next week. Together with May, she went over the homestead and learnt all its secrets including some unlikely things such as how to handle the water tanks. Because they were not connected to town water, they had to rely on rainwater for the house and creek water for the garden.

'There's nothing worse than running out of water and having to get a man to switch tanks for you,' May said as she explained the system.

'Do we often run out of water?'

'Very rarely, it's a huge roof area and the annual rainfall is good, but it's handy to know. It's also somehow become the house responsibility to keep the filters clean, although that's something you won't want to be doing yourself before long. See?'

Both tanks were underground and the business end of them covered with shrubbery as a disguise. 'Just watch out for spiders and snakes,' May added.

Clare swallowed.

'Not that we see many—snakes, I mean. Paddy and Flynn are very good at killing them.'

'I'm so pleased to hear that!'

May smiled at her. 'Come inside—you'll soon get used to the little pinpricks of country life. Frogs in your wellies, cane toads, flying foxes, rabbits—we even get the odd fox—but the bird life is wonderful.'

Clare was much happier to be taught about the house itself and its routine. And over the days she learnt a lot. Who to call if the chimneys smoked, where to get the best firewood, which electrician, plumber and so on Rosemont used in case of any problems. That the first of the month was when Paddy and Flynn got their heart worm and other worm tablets, how often their flea and tick collars needed replacing, how they needed to be brushed every day which was Sean's job.

She learnt how moths were kept at bay in the extensive linen press and how dried, crushed bay leaves were a deterrent to other creepy crawlies.

But it was the inventory of furniture, china and *objets d'art* that fascinated her.

'This Coalport dinner service came out with my grandmother—my grandfather sent for her after he'd been here for five years, would you believe? They weren't married but she waited for him. She also brought out these marvellous old copper warming

pans and fire screens and the grandfather clock. This
Persian rug they picked up when they travelled
through the Middle East. But my father was mostly
responsible for how the house looks today. He was
a great collector of antiques.'

'So—Serena didn't have anything to do with it?'

May grimaced. 'She often said she'd like to re-
model the inside and go more modern. Lachlan
wouldn't let her.'

'What…?' Clare paused and frowned then she
said, 'Sorry, but I can't help myself—what did he
see in her?'

May chewed her lip. 'I often asked myself that,
but I always reminded myself that I liked her a lot
at first. She was…she can be so good with people,
she can be very funny and, believe it or not, she can
be very warm. So, despite the obvious—her sheer
beauty—she didn't seem like a bad choice at first.'

'How long did it take for things to go wrong?'

May sighed. 'She loathed being pregnant, not that
she had a bad time but it obviously cramped her
style. Then—I'm sure she loves Sean in her way, but
she was quite helpless with him. Lachlan handled
him better than she did.'

'Lachlan is a walking encyclopaedia on the joys
and otherwise—*especially* the otherwise—of pregnancy,' Clare said somewhat darkly.

'I'm not surprised. She never let even the mildest
of discomforts escape his notice. You know what I,
personally, found most disturbing about Serena? It
was almost as if she'd made a career—of men.'

Clare blinked.

'Well, she had nothing else to sustain her,' May

explained. 'When she wasn't alluring to them or able to twist them around her little finger, she was disconsolate and unable to turn to anything else or take pleasure in anything else. Her appearance and the effect she had on men was paramount—but then she was a top model.' She shrugged.

'I see,' Clare said slowly.

'Mind you, I don't think Bruce Davidson is going to be a walkover!'

'Funny you should say that, because I had the same feeling— Was that someone at the front door?'

They walked down the main passage together to discover a delivery man on the veranda. Next to him was a large box.

'Uh…' He glanced down at the clipboard in his hand then nervously towards Paddy and Flynn, who might have let him out of his car but were sitting like stern sentinels on either side of the front door. 'Does a Mr Sean Hewitt live here?'

'Well, a Sean Hewitt does live here. What is it?' May enquired.

'Special delivery from Sydney—I need his signature.'

'He's only eight and he's at school. Who's it from?'

'Uh…a B. Davidson, it says here. I guess you can sign for him.'

'It's a telescope!' Clare said, scanning the diagram on the side of the box.

'Sure is.' The delivery man scratched his head. 'And a fine one, too, I'd say, I'd hate to tell you what it's insured for on this trip—you sure he's only eight?'

'I wonder if Lachlan will let him accept it?' May mused a bit anxiously once the delivery man had left.

'Depends on who gets to it first,' Clare responded with a grin. 'I don't think Sean would give it up without a fight. You know—that was rather clever.' And she told May what Bruce had said to her on the subject of Sean.

'It's also bribery of a kind—'

'What is?' Lachlan came round the corner of the house and up the stairs. 'What the hell is this?'

Clare explained and saw an expression of controlled fury cross Lachlan's face. It caused her to sigh inwardly and wonder if these kind of situations were going to become a part of her daily life.

But she gathered herself and said quietly, 'I know it's flamboyant and wickedly expensive but I think he's seriously trying to get to understand Sean better, and that can't be a bad thing.' And she told him what she'd just told May about her conversation with Bruce.

There was utter silence for a long moment. Then Lachlan surprised her immensely. He said, 'On this occasion, I'll trust your judgement, Slim. But you're going to have to do some fast talking if it happens too often.'

'I really don't think it will. I don't think he's— that foolish.'

Lachlan removed his gaze from the container and let it wander idly over her. 'One of the things I like about you is that you're so sane, Mrs Hewitt.' And he held out his hand to her.

May melted into the background.

'You know what's going to happen now, don't

you?' Lachlan said softly as he drew her into his arms.

'I can hazard a guess.' Her lips trembled. 'We're going to be—we're *all* going to become enthusiastic astronomers if only to keep him happy?'

'That too. But I was talking about this.' And he kissed her deeply. Then he lifted his head and looked into her eyes, and said with a look of amusement that took her breath away, 'I don't know if it's my imagination but we seem to be getting farther and farther apart, Slim.'

She rested her hands on his shoulders and looked down at the bulge between them. 'I can't believe it but I'm even growing out of my new maternity clothes!'

'Twins will do that to you every time. When do you see the doctor again?'

Her face changed. 'Why—is something wrong?'

'Not at all, as far as I know, and if you're feeling fine—'

'I am!'

'Well, then, I just asked, that's all,' he said wryly. 'Because I'd like to come with you. Sit down with me for a moment.'

They sat down on the wicker two-seater with its floral cushions and he put an arm round her shoulders.

Clare relaxed. 'I'm supposed to start antenatal classes, too, but you don't have to come to those.'

'Why not?'

'Well, you've been there and done that but, to be honest, I can't think of anything worse.' She grimaced.

He cupped her face. 'I don't blame you. A whole lot of pregnant ladies and their embarrassed husbands is bound to be a bit of a trial. That's why you're better off with me there.'

'Do I really have to do it? I could read up about it.'

He paused. 'As a matter of fact, I haven't been there and done it. Serena refused point-blank to have any truck with antenatal classes. But I often wondered whether it would have made things easier for her.'

'How so?' Clare asked slowly.

'Well, you may not feel so alone, so imposed upon,' he said with a faint grin, 'with the evidence that it's happening to a lot of other women, too. I don't know, but there may be a kind of camaraderie to be found as well. And I'm sure they're designed to take some of the mystery out of the whole process.'

'What if they're all—much younger?' Clare said with obvious misgiving.

'Then we'll be two golden oldies together.'

'You're laughing at me,' she accused.

'I deny the charge completely.'

'All the same I know you are!' She stopped and sighed.

'Why don't you talk to Valerie about it?' he suggested. 'If it's bothering you so much.'

'All right. But I know exactly what she'll say. It's next week, my next appointment.' She told him the date and time.

'The other thing I've been thinking about is—

would you like to ask your parents up for a few days?'

'Lachlan—I'd love to!' Clare sat up enthusiastically. 'My mother's so thrilled about these babies! So's Dad. And you know, it's a strange thing but this—' she put her hands on her stomach '—has brought me closer to my mother than I've ever been before. Not that we weren't close but I feel as if I understand her better now.'

'Why not make it the weekend after next, then?'

She sat back and laid her cheek on his shoulder. 'I will.' And they sat for a while in a silence that was comfortable, warm and peaceful.

Until Paddy and Flynn, who'd been lying at their feet, suddenly leapt up as if of one mind, and started to race down the drive.

'A visitor?' Clare hazarded.

Lachlan shook his head. 'The school bus.'

Clare listened. 'But I can't hear a thing.'

'All the same that's what it will be. They go down to meet Sean every afternoon.'

Clare knew that Sean rode his bicycle down the long drive to the gate every morning and left it there so he could ride it back in the afternoon. She'd never before witnessed Paddy and Flynn racing down the drive to meet him.

But a few minutes later all three appeared, Sean riding his bike like mad as he tried to keep up with the dogs.

'What's this?' he said as he bounded up the veranda steps.

Lachlan explained about the telescope.

For once in his life, Sean Hewitt was struck dumb,

although it only lasted a few moments. Then he said cautiously, 'What have I got to do?'

'Write to him and thank him,' his father said calmly.

'He won't expect me to…go and live with them?'

'I think he might have got that message loud and clear. Why don't you see if there's a note?'

There was, inside the box. It said:

Sorry I treated you like a little kid; the thing is, I don't know much about kids like you or kids at all. But I do know now you're the one kid who could understand and use one of these—have fun; there's no strings attached.

'He may not be such a bad bloke after all,' Sean said after he'd read the note twice.

'You could be right,' Lachlan commented.

Then Sean's sheer joy exploded. 'Dad, have you any idea how I've longed to be able to look at the stars and the moon properly?'

'Well, we've got to assemble it first. I'll give you a hand.'

Clare watched them as they lugged the box inside, then she sat a little longer on the veranda, lapped by a feeling of contentment.

CHAPTER SEVEN

A MONTH sped by.

May departed although she was due back after the babies were born. Sean was so wrapped up in his new telescope he hardly seemed to notice.

With May gone, Clare employed, in addition to the cleaning lady who already came three days a week, another lady to do the laundry and ironing. That virtually left her with only the cooking and she'd always loved to cook. She worked three days a week but always got home around about the same time as Sean.

In fact Sean had so many activities—Cubs, sport and so on—he didn't need entertaining, although he appreciated her help with his homework and the times they spent together at his computer.

He also seemed to appreciate the time they spent together as a family, going to the beach, spending a weekend at Clare's unit, and a kind of camaraderie sprang up between him and Clare. He picked up his father's habit of calling her Slim and didn't mind when she responded by calling him 'kid'.

He also took a keen interest in the whole process of producing babies with his usual mix of *savoir-faire* and tricky questions. And he'd printed out a list of possible names that he kept adding to.

One of the farm staff took over May's beloved rose gardens. He was just as much of an enthusiast as May, and happy to induct Clare into the fragrant business of rose-growing.

All in all, she thought once, the new order of things was working well. Lachlan was deeply into the macadamia harvest and working hard but appeared content, Sean was perfectly happy by the look of it, and she was still in the grip of that curious contentment. She was even beginning to take an interest in the harvest and losing her wariness about the estate. May had been right—country life grew on you, she thought.

Her parents spent a whole week with them and she and her mother had a lovely time designing a nursery. Lachlan went to a lot of trouble to ensure that her father enjoyed his stay, but the person who appreciated Tom Montrose most was Sean. Her father had always been a passionate amateur astronomer.

And Serena and Bruce got married towards the end of the month.

Sean was collected by his maternal grandparents and taken down for the wedding and to spend a few days with them, and he came back obviously impressed. 'You should have seen Serena,' he said to Clare. 'She looked simply smashing! And Bruce couldn't stop smiling. I had a glass of champagne. Yuk! But the food was OK. How's Dad?'

Clare paused because Sean had already been reunited with his father so this question was of a deeper nature, she gathered. 'He's been fine, Sean,' she said honestly.

'Good.' That was all he said but Clare had the feeling they understood each other, she and Sean. Because they had both obviously wondered how

Serena's remarriage would affect Lachlan. But there'd been absolutely nothing to show he'd felt a thing.

And between them Lachlan and Valerie had persuaded Clare to attend some antenatal classes.

Rather to her surprise, because she was expecting twins, Clare was treated like a minor celebrity. Not that it entirely took away her embarrassment, but her sense of humour came to her rescue. There were some first-time fathers present—for the first time—who were obviously ten times more embarrassed than she and unable to disguise their horrified expressions at the video shown of an actual birth.

Even Lachlan said on the way home, 'One doesn't need to be squeamish, does one?'

'No,' Clare agreed ruefully. 'I mean, I've seen them on television before but never in such graphic detail. One suspects that was a very straightforward, easy delivery too.'

He took one hand off the steering wheel and put it over hers. 'I'm quite sure that in this day and age they never let it get too difficult.'

'I hope so. My mother had me in about ten hours and with no stitches and no drugs. I'm just hoping it's genetic—like twins.'

Lachlan was silent for a moment, then he said humorously, 'I need a drink!'

Clare laughed. 'I'm glad!'

'Glad!' He eyed her ruefully.

'Well, I always had the feeling you were such an expert on pregnancy, I—felt a little inadequate by comparison.'

'As a matter of fact, you've coped brilliantly,' he said quietly.

'This may be where it gets tougher, though—the famous—or should it be the notorious?—last trimester.'

'If I'd known what I know now, I'd never have said it,' he murmured.

Clare raised an eyebrow at him.

'Put it this way, it was said in the heat of the moment. And not intended to scare the life out of you.'

'It didn't. Just brought home to me what to expect.'

'You're very forgiving, Clare,' he said quietly.

'Funnily enough, I did get something out of that class,' she said, seemingly changing the subject. 'Other than all the graphic details.'

Lachlan turned into the Rosemont gates. 'You did?'

'Well, there were a couple of lonely-looking single mothers there and there was one girl I had a chat with who was having her fourth in six years, she'd only ever wanted two, her husband is out of work and her parents live overseas. It struck me that I'm very lucky.'

'Because—you have me?'

'Because I have you, I have no financial problems, my parents are only a few hours away, I want these babies—oh, yes, I think so.'

He pulled up in front of the house. But what he'd been going to say was lost as Sean came out to greet them. Although later, in the privacy of their bedroom, he paid her his own tribute.

Winter was fast approaching so they had a fire going and he built it up and warmed some oil in a chafing dish, and massaged her body with slow, gentle fingers, paying attention to her nipples and stopping to laugh softly as his babies did a couple of somersaults.

Then he insisted she put on a fleecy nightgown and robe and they sat in front of the fire and toasted marshmallows.

Finally, he took her to bed and made love to her as if she were precious and breakable. The result was a lovely, warm climax, different from others they'd shared but nonetheless deeply satisfying.

And the next morning when she woke and snuggled up against him she also said, 'That was just what I needed last night. Thanks.'

'Did you think I didn't know?' he responded.

She lifted her head and looked into his eyes with hers a little wondering. 'Know?'

'That there's a time to get technical about pregnancy and babies, and a time to be together like that.'

'That's it, exactly. And from now on antenatal classes will hold no terrors for me.'

He laughed and kissed her. 'Or me. How's work going these days, by the way?'

She told him. 'I've offered Sue a partnership. She's brought in a couple of new clients, quite big ones, and we're thinking of hiring another solicitor. That'll make four of us, though.' She bit her lip. 'I'm just not sure about it. Lennox Head is still only a village really.'

'Have you thought of opening another office? In Ballina or Alstonville?'

She felt a pulse of excitement. 'Would you mind?'

'Well, I don't think you should do it before the babies are born and you've had a chance to settle down, but then—why not?'

'You're right. It's something to think about.'

Things did get tougher from then on as the weeks passed and everything Lachlan had detailed 'in the heat of the moment' came to plague her.

Heartburn, having to get up several times during the night, finding it difficult to get comfortable in bed as she grew bigger and bigger—as well as a few things he hadn't mentioned. How her back ached, for one, although her hair and nails grew and flourished; how difficult it was to get in and out of her sporty little car.

She'd had another scan and although the babies appeared to be fine she was conscious of a niggle of concern that both Valerie and the obstetrician weren't expressing to her.

'Everything's OK, isn't it?' she said one day to Valerie when she had about six weeks to go. Valerie had popped in to see her at work.

Valerie Martin took in the patches of brown pigment on Clare's face, how tired she looked and curiously fragile despite the large burden she carried. 'You should be at home with your feet up,' she said severely.

'I would be but I can't get comfortable even with my feet up,' Clare said ruefully.

Unbeknownst to Clare, it was at Lachlan's instigation that Valerie had popped in to see her. And Valerie decided not to enlighten her but she did ring

Lachlan as soon as she got back to her consulting rooms.

The result of this secret negotiating was that Clare's mother arrived at Rosemont the next morning with the news that she'd come to stay.

'What about Dad? I mean, I'm *thrilled* to have you, but how will he cope?'

'Well, he's just had a check-up and the doctor told him he was fine, the bypass was a great success,' Jane said. 'So I've arranged with a few friends to cook him meals, and the freezer was pretty well stocked anyway, but he'll come up on weekends. He'll probably enjoy having free access to the bowls club anyway! In the meantime we can put the finishing touches to the nursery and the layette!'

But Jane Montrose did more. She insisted on helping with the cooking and with someone there to talk to and knit, sew and crochet with Clare was happier to stay at home.

Towards the end of her eighth month, on a visit to the obstetrician, that niggle of unspoken concern was at last brought out into the open.

'Clare,' he said to her, 'there's a possibility this pregnancy won't go full term.'

She looked at him wide-eyed.

'Firstly,' he said, 'around sixty per cent of twins are born a few weeks early so from now on you should have all your arrangements made. Secondly, pre-eclampsia is more common when you're carrying twins so if there's *any* sign of fluid retention, dizziness, blurred vision or headaches you must let us know immediately, and we'll need to be vigilant with your blood pressure.'

'I haven't noticed anything like that.'

'Good,' he said. 'But the other thing is, in light of your mother's history of one twin not surviving, we need to monitor their condition closely. If either foetus seems at all distressed, we'll need to do a Caesarean.'

'I'd much rather do this naturally,' she said.

'Believe me, so would I. I'm not in favour of routine Caesareans but they can be life- and health-saving. The other thing is the burden on *you*, now and at delivery. There's just a touch of concern about your pelvic measurements. Now, I've known little slips of girls who've produced seven- and eight-pound babies with ease but you were very slim and I don't propose to endanger you or your babies if things look difficult.'

'I...see.'

'As for monitoring you—three,' he said with a glint of humour, 'Valerie has offered to pop in every day on her way to work. Apparently she drives past Rosemont. So she can check their heartbeats, your blood pressure and so on. The alternative is to put you into hospital—'

'Oh, no, I—'

'I thought not,' he said wryly. 'But, Clare, believe me, if that does have to happen, it's a small price to pay for two healthy babies and a healthy mum!'

She told Lachlan of this development as soon as she got home.

She drove down to the sorting shed to find him and he must have sensed something from her expression because he immediately left the conveyor belt that was pouring a river of nuts into a small silo and led her outside to a wooden bench beneath a gnarled old fig tree.

It was a crisp, cool morning and the vista before them fled away in tones of blue and gold, blue sky, winter-gold grass bisected by the orderly rows of dark green macadamia trees.

'What's up, Slim?' He threaded his fingers through hers. 'You look very serious.'

She told him.

'Ah. So he decided to tell you.'

She blinked at him. 'Decided…do you mean you already knew?'

'I—let's say I had an inkling so I spoke to Valerie, and she already had these things on her mind. So we conferred with the obstetrician but decided not to worry you because there may be nothing to worry about anyway. And he suggested that he would only bring it up if he thought it was necessary at this consultation so you would be better prepared.'

'I can't believe it,' Clare said ominously. 'What am I—a sixteen-year-old kid?'

He looked at her in her enormous berry-red wool jumper and navy skirt. Then he laughed and kissed her knuckles. 'No, although you don't look much older sometimes, but you are a very pregnant lady with enough on her plate as it is.'

'I suppose—I suppose you organized my mother as well!'

'Believe me, when I rang her she said she'd been dying to do it anyway but she hadn't wanted to interfere.'

Clare digested this. 'And Valerie?'

'She's very fond of you, Clare. She offered to do it. Any more objections?'

All at once, Clare felt guilty. 'No. I...no. Thanks. I just—'

'Don't like to be the one not making the decisions?'

She sighed. 'It sounds churlish, doesn't it?'

'The thing is, whatever happens, my dear Slim, we're all there behind you, and you're not to worry.'

She laid her head on his shoulder and so badly wanted to say 'I love you', she had to bite her lip. She also slipped into the little world that had been her refuge at these times—she put her hands on her stomach and concentrated her thoughts on her babies. It worked and she didn't notice Lachlan watching her bent head with a frown in his eyes.

She had a long rest after lunch but couldn't sleep as she contemplated all sorts of things.

She'd discovered in the last weeks a tendency to be morbidly sensitive, and although she knew it was common to late pregnancy it wasn't any less real. Anything violent or sad, especially to do with children, affected her far more than usual.

Strange dreams sometimes plagued her sleep but today it was thoughts about the coming birth that filled her mind. A Caesarean, for one, obviously less arduous than a natural birth but, from her reading and antenatal classes, not as easily recovered from because it was, after all, major surgery. Breech births—she'd read about the consequences of those.

Babies with dislocated hips who had to wear a brace for months. She shivered involuntarily.

Her thoughts wandered on to natural births, and the often read comment that all the antenatal classes, all the exercises, practising breathing and measures you could take to relax didn't really prepare you for the pain involved.

She moved restlessly and deliberately switched her thoughts to Lachlan who couldn't have been better in these last difficult weeks. He'd surrounded her with care, he knew instinctively when sex was the last thing she wanted although she loved the warmth and reassurance of his solid bulk behind her in bed.

Lachlan, who also had never said that he loved her—perhaps he didn't think it needed saying, she mused.

But a strange compulsion grew within her to find some way of expressing *her* feelings. She wondered if it was prompted by dire thoughts of Caesareans or the ordeal of a natural birth.

She got up, found a writing pad and pen, sat in front of the fire in her bedroom, and started to write. She began conventionally enough:

Dear Lachlan,
How to tell you I love you? Perhaps I can only go back to the beginning. I think my love for you was always there. That's why I had those strange bouts of uneasiness I couldn't put a name to. It all seemed so suitable, our affair, while we made no demands on each other and were so adult and modern.

So when did it hit me that I loved you, rather than hovering in my subconscious? When I told you I was pregnant, although I had more than an inkling, I suspect, because it was extraordinarily hard to tell you about the baby. Why? I didn't know where I stood, I didn't know if I was your way of getting over Serena. I just knew there was a part of you that was a closed book to me.

And when I did tell you about the baby, although you offered to marry me straight away, I still couldn't read your mind completely—and that's when it really hit me that I loved you.

To be honest, the only reason I seemed determined then to be a single mum was because it hurt me to know that you didn't love me as I loved you. It's funny that, isn't it? I mean, despite being so career-oriented, in hindsight, I don't think I was cut out to be a single parent at all, or even much of a feminist—but that's just by the way.

Why did you ask me to marry you? I've asked myself that a hundred times. Was it because of Sean? Was it out of a sense of duty because I was pregnant? Perhaps both—I still don't know but I do sense that there's something unfinished between you and Serena, like dark waters lapping silently, and that there's some territory you may never be able to let me into. That's why I haven't told you this before and may never tell you.

Why do I love you? You always did take my breath away; you released a side of me I didn't know existed but it's like the ocean beneath my windows at Lennox now. It's a vast source of pleasure, to be your lover, to laugh with you, to live with you, to know that my life would always be bleak and cheerless without you. To want these two babies for one simple reason—because they're ours.

She put her pen down and rubbed her eyes. But the tears continued to fall. Then she took some deep breaths and discovered she felt better. As if she'd at least resolved her own feelings and could go forward to whatever was in front of her with a clearer mind.

She found an envelope, put the letter in it and sealed it, then wrote his name on it and slipped it beneath her underwear in a drawer.

And went out to welcome Sean home from school.

A few days later Lachlan told her that Serena had rung because the school holidays were almost upon them and because she and Bruce were again in the district they'd like to take Sean away for a while.

'What does he think?'

'He doesn't seem to mind. Apparently Bruce maintains a unit and a boat on the Gold Coast and they're planning a few days cruising in Moreton Bay. Sean's seen pictures of the boat and is very impressed.'

'Well, that's good,' Clare said. 'I mean, that hunger strikes et cetera have faded from his mind,' she added humorously, but she sobered almost immediately. 'How do *you* feel about it?'

She was lying propped up on a settee in the den with her feet in his lap and he was massaging them. It was about nine in the evening and her mother and Sean were both in bed.

'I don't have much choice,' he said after a moment. 'But I'm still trusting to your judgement on the subject.'

She smiled faintly. 'I think you may also be able

to trust Bruce's judgement on the subject. After all, no more exotic gifts have arrived but Sean obviously feels more comfortable with him now. And look how much pleasure he still gets out of his telescope.'

'I'm looking. Do you realize I can almost identify every damn thing in the Milky Way?'

'Well, there are compensations,' she murmured, and sighed. 'That's lovely.'

'I'm glad, but I don't see the connection between your poor feet and the Milky Way.'

'No—that just slipped in,' she said with a grin. 'I meant—the Nez Percé stage was not only noisy and messy but a great trial to Paddy and Flynn.'

'Ah, but I'm not Paddy or Flynn!'

'You know what I mean.'

'Yes.' He laid his head back. 'They want to come and pick him up the day after tomorrow.'

Clare was silent.

He raised his head. 'But if you'd rather not I can—'

'No. No. We might as well do all we can to make things easy for Sean. Ask them to come for lunch.'

'Clare, you don't have to do that and especially not now.'

She grimaced. 'I can still cope with a luncheon. And if you've never seen my mother on her mettle, her domestic mettle, you're in for a treat.' She stopped and yawned.

'If you say so,' he said slowly, then, 'Bedtime, Mrs Hewitt.'

'I'm afraid so but you don't have to come.'

He helped her up and stood with his hands resting

lightly on her shoulders before he said, 'Are you saying you don't want me to come?'

'No, of course not. I just know you don't normally come to bed at these early hours and—'

'Things have changed. And I want to make sure you get comfortable and get to sleep—for a while anyway,' he said with a glint of amusement. 'A back rub seems to do the trick.'

'Lachlan,' she said on a breath, 'you're...you've been so wonderful, I don't know how to thank you.'

He looked down at her and was struck as Valerie had been by her fragility and the shadows under her eyes. And he found himself wondering how she'd borne this pregnancy, carried the heavy burden of twins, let alone all that had happened between them, and undertaken the change of life-style so bravely.

The question that was beginning to torment him more and more was—why? Was she, against all expectations, a born mother? Was that what sustained her? Or had she guessed the heart of his dilemma, the things that had held him back—the memories that still plagued him of his first marriage?

He said at last, 'Don't thank me, Clare. You've been brave and beautiful and it's only a month at the most now. Come.'

It was a cold, wet day, the day Bruce and Serena were coming to pick up Sean, so Clare and Jane laid out lunch in the dining room.

'I must say this seems a little odd but at the same time I think you're doing the right thing by Sean,' Jane said. 'What's she like?'

'Very beautiful. But I don't think she likes me.

Still, it was their idea to come to pick up Sean—or perhaps it was Bruce's idea? He's pretty sane. How do I look?'

'Darling...' Jane paused and Clare started to laugh.

'Don't answer that—very pregnant!'

'Actually I was going to say that you look fine. For a few days there you were looking a bit peaky but you've got your glow back again. And that outfit becomes you.'

The outfit in question was a fine black wool trouser suit with a tunic top and a little ruff around the neck edged with silver. Some judicious make-up had covered up the brown patches on her face and her hair, in its usual curly bob, was dark and shiny. Her nails were beautifully manicured and painted to match the berry-red of her lips. She wore black patent shoes with little silver heels.

'You know, you're lucky you're tall, too,' her mother continued. 'You got that from your father. I'm only five feet two and by the time I was eight months pregnant I truly looked like a blob on the landscape, whereas you look quite regal.'

Clare regarded the large bulge of her stomach that was obscuring her feet, and came round the table to kiss her mother lightly on the brow. 'You're sweet.'

But Lachlan confirmed her mother's words. 'Why, Slim,' he said, 'you look like a million quid!'

'One has to fight fire...the best way one knows how,' she said honestly, and ignored his quizzical little look. 'I think I heard a car.'

Clare was bemused because this Serena couldn't have been more different from the Serena of their first encounter.

And she found herself remembering what May had said—how good Serena could be with people, how warm...

She was just that. She went out of her way to charm Jane Montrose, she was playful and affectionate with Sean, she exhibited proper wifely closeness towards Bruce—and she swapped pregnancy experiences with Clare as if she were a good friend.

As a potentially difficult lunch party, not to mention a minefield, it was neither. Conversation flowed, as did the good food and wine, and, to top it off, Serena was so exquisitely beautiful, so slim yet rounded in all the right places in a suede dress that matched her cornflower-blue eyes, it was hard to take one's eyes off her.

Bruce was certainly unable to for long, although once Clare thought she detected a glint of something a little dry in his gaze.

And Lachlan did, a couple of times, allow his gaze to rest narrowly but enigmatically on his ex-wife.

Then it was time to leave, and it all suddenly fell into place for Clare.

Serena laid a light hand on her stomach and said sweetly, 'You poor thing—I know what it's like when you *feel* like a bean bag and wonder if you can ever return to normal. Good luck!'

She turned to Lachlan and simply stood quite still for a moment, inviting his gaze upon her slender figure, and when their eyes clashed she smiled a brief, secret little smile as she murmured goodbye, and went to put her arm through Bruce's.

Go and find that letter and tear it up, was the thought that flooded Clare's mind as Lachlan stood straight and tall beside her, almost as if he weren't breathing.

Sean created a much needed diversion at that point by suddenly deciding he'd forgotten to pack his togs.

'No, you haven't,' Clare said calmly. 'We packed two pairs—remember?'

'Gosh—you're right, Slim!' he said, and put his arms around her as far as they would go. 'Listen, don't have these babies before I get back! I want to be in on the ground floor.'

She patted his head, more grateful than he could ever know, and said gravely, 'I'll try not to. Have fun, kid.'

They watched them drive off and Lachlan turned to say something to Clare, but his foreman drove up with a squeal of tyres in the estate utility with the news that a fire had broken out in the sorting shed.

'You'd better go,' Clare said naturally. 'It sounds pretty serious.'

He hesitated and watched her narrowly for a moment. Then a siren made itself heard, and he turned away with a muttered curse.

When he got back late that evening—he'd rung through a couple of times to let them know how it was going and reassure them he was in no danger—Jane greeted him with the news that Clare had gone to bed.

'I think she was exhausted, poor thing. It might be an idea not to disturb her. Rest is really important for her now.'

Lachlan hesitated then looked down at the mess he was in. 'I'll sleep in a spare room.'

The next morning Clare was amazed to discover that she'd slept for hours, deeply and dreamlessly. She turned her head to discover she was alone and, from the unrumpled other side of the bed, realized she had been alone all night.

She lay back and thought about it. The common-sense answer was that he hadn't wanted to disturb her, she reasoned. But the idea that he couldn't get Serena out of his mind was also there.

Not that there was a thing she could do about it, she mused.

A few minutes later she got up, pulled on her robe and went to find him.

He was fast asleep in a spare bedroom but the opening of the door woke him, and as she stood there he stared at her, blinking sleepily, then he got up so fast he knocked over the bedside table complete with lamp and a couple of books as well as a phone.

'Is it— Clare, are they coming?' he said rapidly, and tripped over the phone cord to get himself tangled up in the frill of the bedcover. He was also stark naked.

She couldn't help the gurgle of laughter that rose as he extricated himself from the frill and pushed his tawny hair out of his eyes impatiently. 'No—sorry— no, it's not. I thought I'd lost you, that's all.'

He heaved a sigh of relief then looked at her severely. 'I gather I made a bit of a spectacle of myself.' He began to restore the table and its contents.

'A bit,' she agreed, still unable to keep a straight

face. 'Regrettably, the fact that you have no clothes on seems to heighten the comic aspect of it.'

He came over to her and stood with his hands on his hips. 'I have no clothes on because I didn't want to wake you last night, Mrs Hewitt, and even my underwear smelled of smoke. You may have forgotten that I was tending a fire?'

'Mr Hewitt, my abject apologies.' This time she managed to sound sober. 'But you were also very sweet.'

'Clare, I wish you wouldn't do that!'

She raised an innocent eyebrow.

'Call me sweet! It makes me feel entirely harmless—and cuddly.'

'I do like to cuddle you,' she murmured. 'Shall I show you?'

'It'll have to be a pretty good demo because my feelings are very hurt.' He looked at her with an entirely false expression of wounded pride—a little glint she knew well in his eyes gave him away.

'Oh, I think I could manage that,' she said, and undid her robe. 'Come back to bed.'

'Clare—'

'I wouldn't talk either, if I were you,' she added.

'No?'

'No. Just relax and let me do all the…talking.'

Not many minutes later, he shuddered in release and she kissed him lightly on the lips and ran her fingers through his hair.

'Why did you do that?' he asked huskily. 'Not that I'm complaining, it was wonderful, but…'

Why had she? Clare wondered. To lay the spectre

of Serena? No, it had seemed to come quite naturally; Serena had never entered her mind.

'I couldn't help myself,' she said softly. 'And you deserve it, to make up for all the times I didn't feel like it.'

'You're—' he paused then grinned wickedly at her '—sweet.'

'Then we're even!'

'I don't know about that. Clare—' the smile died out of his eyes '—about yesterday.'

'Lachlan, I told you not to worry about Serena.' She looked tranquilly into his eyes.

He paused. 'But—'

'No.' She put a finger on his lips. 'I feel so remarkably well today, anyway—did the fire do much damage?'

He sank back. 'Half the shed will have to be rebuilt but we managed to save all the nuts.'

'How did it start?'

'Don't know yet. It could have been an electrical overload or a surge of some kind. One of the machines has also been playing up and overheating but I thought we'd fixed it. No one was actually in the shed when it started but it's going to put us back a fair bit.'

'Are you insured?'

'Yes,' he said a shade grimly. 'When one gets down to the fine print, however, you can be in for some unpleasant surprises.'

'You seem to forget,' she said humorously.

'What?'

'That you have your own tame lawyer who even

goes to bed with you.' Her eyes danced but her de-
meanour was decorous.

'So I did,' he said slowly. 'You're not only my
legal wife, you're a very legal kind of wife!'

'Which is not to say that I can get you more than
you're entitled to—'

'Perish the thought!'

'On the other hand, I can interpret the fine print
when a mere layman is often overwhelmed by it.'

'Mere?'

'Well, you know what I mean!'

'I know you're very full of yourself this morning,
Mrs Hewitt.'

'Not only that,' she said gravely, 'fully occupied
within myself. There doesn't seem a corner to spare.'

He put his hand on her stomach and laughed down
at her. 'If that's the cause of all this, then I forgive
you. Wow! A bit of activity going on in here.'

'They had such a peaceful night they could be
making up for it. By the way, I'm starving.'

'Now you mention it so am I. Shall we breakfast
royally?'

'Why not?'

Her feeling of well-being lasted through the day and
into the next. Valerie paid her daily visit and said to
Clare and Lachlan the following morning, 'You
know, this is all looking so good, I'm inclined to
think you will go full term, Clare. Which is all the
better for the babies—but don't take *any* chances, of
course! So—what have we got? About three weeks?'

Clare groaned.

'*Rest,*' Valerie and Lachlan said in unison.

'I know, I know. And I will! Bring me your insurance policies, Mr Hewitt. I might as well be useful even while I'm resting.'

CHAPTER EIGHT

THE next morning Lachlan came pounding up the veranda steps. Then Clare, who was in the lounge that opened onto the veranda, saw him stop abruptly, take a deep breath and walk along the veranda more normally.

She went out to greet him anxiously and saw that he was pale. 'What is it?'

'Clare...' he hesitated '...come and sit down.'

'But something's happened. I saw you—not another fire?'

'No.' He led her to a chair. 'It's—well, I got a call from Bruce, I gave them my mobile number. Apparently they were anchored at Jumpinpin on the Broadwater last night and this morning some unlicensed idiot in an out-of-control aluminium dinghy rammed and holed their boat—'

'Oh, no!' she whispered, going white herself. 'Sean?'

'Hang on. Their boat started to sink, it's a fibreglass hull, and in the drama that followed Serena broke her leg and Sean banged his head and knocked himself out. Now, they think he's OK but to be on the safe side they're airlifting them all to the Gold Coast Hospital and they're going to do some tests on Sean.'

'You must go,' she said immediately.

Lachlan looked supremely frustrated and swore

beneath his breath. 'How can I leave you? It couldn't have happened at a worse possible time.'

'Lachlan—' she took his hands in hers '—you heard what Valerie said yesterday and it's only a two-hour drive to Southport and the Gold Coast Hospital. I'll be fine and I won't be alone anyway—not that anything is going to happen today. Please, I couldn't bear it if Sean was asking for you and you weren't there.'

Still he hesitated. 'You can't *know* anything isn't going to happen today.'

'Well, no, but my intuition tells me it won't. I feel so well, I even feel reconciled to this whale-like version of me so I guess I am going to go full term.'

He cupped her face suddenly and kissed her. 'You're a brick, but don't forget if there's the slightest twinge ring me. I'll be back by this evening, anyway.'

She and her mother ate lunch; there was no news yet. Then Clare stood up to start clearing the table—and frowned.

'What is it, dear?'

Clare looked at her watch.

'Clare!' Jane stood up, clutching her napkin.

'I think,' her daughter said dazedly, 'that may have been a contraction.'

'Not a Braxton Hicks contraction?'

'It felt different.' She swallowed and sat down again then immediately stood up. 'If it is, standing upright is better for the cervix or something, but how can we tell the difference? I know, the real contractions are regular,' she answered herself, and discovered that she was trembling from head to toe. 'But I was feeling so fine!'

'Oh, I wondered about that,' Jane said distractedly as she reached for the phone. 'I washed every curtain in the house the day before you were born but I've never been sure whether it was an old wives' tale.'

Clare held onto the back of her chair. 'Who are you ringing?'

'Lachlan, of course.'

'Mum, hang on a moment, please, this may be a false alarm—'

'But he made me promise—'

'Just let's wait a bit, please,' Clare begged.

Jane hesitated. 'Then let me ring Valerie.'

'All right…'

Clare had had another contraction by the time Valerie came on the phone, fifteen minutes after the first, but she said to Valerie, 'I can't help wondering if it's a false alarm, I've read that it's really common, especially with first babies, but it is different from all the other aches and pains—'

'Clare, get yourself into the hospital on the double; I'll meet you there,' Valerie said authoritatively.

'I'm ringing him first, I don't care what you say.' Jane also became authoritative. But, to her dismay, Lachlan's mobile was either switched off or in a non-mobile area. 'Damn!' she said. 'He could be in the hospital. They don't allow mobiles in the wards, I remember from when your father was there. Never mind, I'll try again when we get there. Now, have we got everything?'

She looked around the colourful chaos of Clare's

bedroom—they'd been tidying out Clare's wardrobe before lunch—and grimaced. 'Never mind, it can all wait. Let's go, darling! But first let me hug you and tell you how much I love and admire you!'

'Clare, you're definitely in labour, the cervix is dilating, but there's no way of knowing at this stage how long it's going to take. Because it's twins we're going to put you in a labour ward so we can monitor them continually. How are you feeling?'

'Not too bad, if it doesn't get worse than this I'll be OK.'

Valerie glanced at the obstetrician over Clare's head then said to her, 'You try to rest and relax. Sure you're warm enough? I'll get the sister to bring you a heating pad for your poor feet, they're icy! Oh, and your mother is trying to get hold of Lachlan. His phone's still out so she's ringing the Gold Coast Hospital.'

They wheeled her into the labour ward and made her as comfortable as possible. There was some discussion about hooking her up to an EFM machine but they decided to wait for a while because both babies' heartbeats were normal, and it would restrict her from moving around.

The truth be told, she thought, she couldn't believe this was finally happening to her and she didn't know whether she was scared witless or in shock.

She had on a hospital nightgown that opened down the back, a pair of socks, and was covered by a white cotton blanket. She also had a name tag on her wrist and they'd tied her hair back in a ponytail. There were two humidicribs lined up against one wall.

For a short time she rested comfortably, feeling the rhythmic surge of her contractions and wondering where Lachlan was, how Sean was.

They came and checked the babies' heartbeats frequently and asked her once whether she would be more comfortable standing or walking around—perhaps she'd like a warm shower?—but she told them she was quite comfortable as she was.

Then her mother came and sat with her for a while and imparted the news that she still hadn't reached Lachlan himself but she'd left messages everywhere she could think of for him.

'But I finally managed to speak to Bruce,' she went on, 'and the good news is that Sean is suffering from a mild concussion, that's all. Serena does have a broken leg but it's a simple fracture.'

'Doesn't Bruce know where Lachlan is?' Clare asked drowsily.

'He was with them but Bruce thinks he tried to ring home and when he got no answer decided to drive down straight away. In which case he'll be here pretty soon, darling!'

Not soon enough as it turned out. Because barely had her mother spoken those words than a severe contraction gripped Clare and the pain almost made her feel like fainting.

'Mum—'

'It's OK, I'll get them.'

'Oh-ho!' the obstetrician said as he examined her a few minutes later. 'No fooling around for the Hewitt twins. Clare, you're fully dilated, my dear, and you'll be feeling like pushing very shortly— we're with you every inch of the way!'

The labour ward suddenly became a hive of activity. A nurse stood beside her wiping her brow and with a nitrous oxide mask ready. Another attended to the cribs. Valerie was there holding her hand and talking to her all the time.

But all Clare could think was that she'd been right: nothing fully prepared you for labour; the pain was crushing and when it let you go you prayed for it not to come back but it always did. Then she told them hoarsely that she wanted to push and they said that was wonderful, fine, just to do as they said and not to forget to pant like a dog when they told her; they needed to take this gently...

Gently? she thought as her face contorted. They must be kidding! But she alternately pushed and panted and felt as if she was about to split open.

'Way to go!' the obstetrician finally said gleefully. 'We have a touch-down. A boy! What did I tell you about little slips of girls?'

'Oh! Oh!' was all Clare could say, because after the briefest respite it started again.

'Honey, you're doing a treat,' the nurse beside her said as Valerie went to the baby, 'and by the look of it here comes Dad!'

'Lachlan,' Clare wept as he loomed up beside her in a gown and a cap. 'Oh, thank heavens! But I've done it once, I can do it again.'

And she did. Ten minutes later, with his arms around her and saying things to her he'd never said before, a little girl entered the world.

'How are they—are they all right? Oh, look at them!' She was crying, but they were tears of joy and relief. 'Are they all right?'

They put them into her arms. 'They're fine, Clare, as far as we can tell. Not big babies but they look to be perfect.'

'Were we ever wrong about you, Clare!' Valerie said, laughing. 'That was about three and a half hours from start to finish!'

Several hours later Clare was resting comfortably in her pretty room although her babies were in the nursery in humidicribs. At five and five and a half pounds respectively and with some indications that they were slightly premature—peeling skin, for example—it had been decided to do that just to be on the safe side. But the obstetrician had assured Clare and Lachlan they were fine.

She and Lachlan were alone, for her mother had tactfully gone home. And Clare was still on an incredible high. 'I just can't stop smiling,' she said to Lachlan. 'I feel like telling the whole world I did it!'

'You did,' he said. 'All on your own.'

She grimaced. 'So much for my intuition!'

He explained how he'd had to switch his mobile off while he was with Sean and then, once he'd got out of the ward, how all he'd got when he'd rung home was the phone ringing out.

'We forgot to put on the answering machine, we could have put another message on it. I just didn't think,' Clare said ruefully.

'I'm not surprised, but my thumbs started to prickle immediately,' he said. 'I kept telling myself you'd probably just gone out to do some shopping and forgotten about the answering machine but I couldn't quite believe it.'

Clare had spoken to Sean on the phone as well as Bruce—they were going to release Sean the next day and Lachlan would pick him up. Bruce had said that Serena was resting as comfortably as possible, and he'd congratulated Clare enthusiastically.

'Now all we've got to do is work out names,' Clare said to Lachlan. 'I'm so glad one is a girl, I'd have been pretty heavily outnumbered otherwise.'

He smiled at her. 'I love you.'

She stared into his eyes, suddenly arrested. 'You said that...you said it while...'

'I know.' He closed his eyes briefly then looked at her with clear pain etched in them. 'If you only knew—I'll never forgive myself for not saying it sooner.'

'Did...was it the birth?' she asked shakily.

'No. It was because I was never sure how you felt—until I found this.' He pulled something out of the inside pocket of his tweed sports coat.

Clare gasped as she recognized it—her letter. 'I...I was going to tear that up.'

'Thank God you didn't.'

'How did you find it?'

'As soon as I arrived home I went tearing into our bedroom. For a moment I thought you'd decided to leave me—there were clothes everywhere. The drawer this was in was open and it caught my eye.'

Clare sighed. 'We were sorting through everything, Mum and I, putting away things I mightn't be able to wear for a while.'

'Can I answer the questions you raised in here, Clare?'

After a moment, she nodded.

'There is nothing unfinished between me and Serena, not on my side—but yes, she did leave me with some dark waters to cope with.'

He looked into the distance then back into her eyes. 'It's particularly hard to have to admit that you got taken in by a face and a body but that's what happened to me. It was as if she'd cast a spell over me so that I ignored all the warning signs. The little signs that told me I might not be able to transform this glamorous creature, so used to the high life and all the adulation of being a top model, into a country wife.'

Clare moved a little then subsided.

'But as the marriage progressed I learnt that wasn't all that I'd misjudged. I told you once that when the chips were down the only thing that mattered to Serena was Serena—that's true but it was worse. She used her body to get her own way. She played on my infatuation and even when it began to fade she traded herself—I can only call it that—in a way that eventually nauseated me. And a few days ago she was still trying to do it.'

Clare stared at him wide-eyed. 'I thought—I mean, I saw it with my own eyes but I thought—'

'You thought she'd got to me?' he supplied.

'You went so still,' Clare whispered.

'I know. Still with the effort not to tell her that she was a slut and a whore, that I'd never loved her as I loved you, and that I now knew the difference between a good woman and the type she was.'

Clare blinked and licked her lips. 'That was part of the...dark waters?' she asked.

'I'm afraid so. Once a fool, always a fool, perhaps,

but when you've been manipulated by a beautiful woman you become wary. I'm sorry. But you put that theory—that all women are the same—to rest when you got so blazingly angry with me one night. Do you remember?'

'I...oh, yes,' she breathed, her mind racing back to the row they'd had over May leaving. 'It was as if you were waiting for something. Then, the next morning, you were—'

'Playful and sweet?' he suggested ruefully.

'You thought...?' She stopped.

'I was waiting to see whether you would use the kind of tricks Serena used to get your own way.' He frowned frustratedly. 'Not really consciously but when I thought about it I knew damn well what I'd been doing.'

'Oh,' Clare said hoarsely. 'Why didn't you tell me then?'

'My darling—' he picked up her hand and kissed her knuckles '—there's more. Are you feeling OK, though? This might not be the best time—'

'Lachlan, there's never going to be a better time.'

He flinched visibly. 'If only I could have told you this before but...' he paused '...the thing is, from the time I first met you, Clare, I was attracted to you, and as I got to know you I realized—except for insane moments like that night—that there was no way I could compare you to Serena except in one respect.'

'Go on,' she said huskily. 'But I think I know what you mean.'

'I kept asking myself if I'd done it again—made an unsuitable choice, fallen for someone who would no more fit in or want to fit in with my life-style and Rosemont than she had.'

'I...I probably didn't help. I did genuinely think my career was all-important at that stage of my life,' she said with a stricken little look.

'No, you didn't help,' he said slowly. 'You seemed so perfectly satisfied with that "no strings attached" kind of relationship—'

'Secretly I wasn't, though. As the months passed I—but I didn't think you wanted to be pinned down.'

He fiddled with her wedding ring. 'It's crazy, isn't it? I did but I didn't. Can you forgive me?'

She sniffed and blinked.

'But when the opportunity came to—pin *you* down, Clare, I couldn't resist it and I began to realize why. I couldn't begin to think of living without you even though I had grave fears of how it was going to turn out. It was a compulsion that even overrode my fears of what a second unsuccessful marriage would do to Sean. So, no, it wasn't because of him that I did it.'

She gazed at him, unable to speak.

'I know what you're thinking—how *well* it turned out so why didn't I say something sooner? But I still couldn't be sure—why it was working.'

'What do you mean?'

'I saw it happen for the first time on the last night of our honeymoon. I thought, There she goes again, slipping away from me, only it isn't work now, it's her babies. I felt excluded, I felt that they were very real for you and the rest of it might just be a case of you lying in the bed you'd made and making the best of it that you could.'

Clare swallowed then burst into tears.

'Sweetheart, don't.' He put his arms around her and kissed her hair. 'Because if it's like a vast ocean for you, if I ever took your breath away, I couldn't have loved you more when you were huge and tired but always so brave, and I'll never stop loving you.'

'I only slipped away because I was so unsure of you—oh, we've been at such cross purposes,' she wept.

'I know,' he said broodingly. 'And it's all my fault but—' he kissed her tears '—if it hasn't come too late, Clare, you've restored my faith, you're my joy, my peace, my partner. And I had planned to tell you all this tonight whatever the consequences. Because I knew I couldn't let you go through *this* without knowing how I felt even if it didn't mean all that much to you.'

He paused and grimaced. 'Two little people had other ideas, however. Not to mention fires, boating accidents—I can't imagine what else could have happened in the last couple of days!'

'Lachlan,' she said urgently, 'I love you. And it means the world to me. If only *you* knew how often I've wanted to say it.'

Some time later a nurse pushing a wheelchair disturbed them.

'Now, that is nice,' she said cheerily as they drew apart. 'Always like to see the mums and dads having a bit of a cuddle, but would you like to come down to the nursery? Your babies are awake and could also do with a bit of a cuddle.'

They were not only awake and out of their cribs,

they were crying. 'Here,' the nurse said as she handed one bundle to Clare and one to Lachlan. 'See what you can do.'

The pink bundle Lachlan held immediately stopped crying.

'Don't you dare be better at this than I am!' Clare said to him, but she was laughing. 'Oh, look, he's stopped, too,' she added as the blue bundle in her arms yawned mightily then composed himself for sleep.

And they sat side by side comparing their babies.

'They're almost identical!' Lachlan said. 'How are we going to tell them apart other than the obvious?'

'Well, she's smaller for a start and I think her hair—they've got your hair!' Clare said wonderingly, running her fingers over the gingery down. 'But hers is a little fairer. And they can't be identical because they're fraternal twins, otherwise they'd be the same sex.'

'I bow to your greater knowledge. But I think they both look a lot like you.'

'How can you tell?' Clare asked, fascinated. 'If anything, I think they look like you.'

'It's always hard to know if someone looks like one self,' he said gravely.

'Believe it or not,' the nurse said, 'if you had six different people in here they'd have six different ideas on who they look like.'

'We believe you,' Clare and Lachlan chorused, and they all laughed.

'OK, names,' he said then.

'Are we agreed on Tom for this young man?' Clare kissed her son's forehead.

'We are—how about Thomas Paul? Paul was my father's name.'

'Oh, that's one of Sean's favourites, so yes! What was your mother's name?'

'Anna.'

'How about Anna-Jane?'

'Done,' he replied promptly, and said to the baby in his arms, 'Now, young Anna-Jane Hewitt, this is your father speaking. I do think you could at least open your eyes!'

But Anna-Jane only copied her brother. She yawned, waved an incredibly small fist, and fell asleep again.

'Bed for you now, too, Mrs Hewitt,' the nurse said. 'You've had a very big day. We'll bring them in to you first thing in the morning!' she added as Clare looked reluctant.

'Will you sleep?' Lachlan said to her when she was tucked in.

'I wish I had you to cuddle up to.'

He watched her carefully for a moment and wondered how to help her relax and not tumble down from the clouds of euphoria too drastically.

Then he pulled a chair up beside the bed, put his feet up and began rhythmically to stroke her hair. 'Do you remember Orpheus?'

'Mmm... It was lovely.'

'So were you. Like a flower in bloom, a golden creature with eyes like the sea and midnight hair. And sweet, even when you were wondering what you'd let yourself in for.'

'You mean your shirts?' she said drowsily.

'Not only my shirts but what a big bad wolf I might turn out to be.'

She chuckled sleepily. 'I didn't go that far.'

He smiled faintly. 'On our first night you were definitely concerned but—did I prove you wrong?'

She moved but it was like a luxurious settling of her weary and sore body. 'If you thought I was— nice, I thought you were—not sweet,' she murmured. 'Like a splendid tiger, lithe and strong, so strong but nice, too.'

'Well, it's my turn to be strong again,' he said gently. 'And it's your turn to go to sleep because I'll be here all night right beside you and ready for our babies in the morning.'

'You don't—'

'I want to, my darling—you know, I was right about one thing.'

'Oh?'

'I suspected you were a born mother!'

She laughed softly. 'Against all expectations—I've surprised myself...'

He said no more and a few minutes later her breathing told him she was asleep. But it was an hour or more before he closed his eyes as he kept stroking her hair and willing her to get the rest she so richly deserved. At the same time he was thinking his own thoughts, remembering her as a cool, clever solicitor and contrasting that image with all she'd become. A warm, wonderful woman, now a mother but, above all, his own.

When she woke at daylight, he was asleep in the chair beside her.

She looked her fill. His chin was resting on his

shoulder, his hands were clasped in his lap. There were blue shadows on his jaw and his tawny hair was falling across his forehead. He still had his feet propped up on the bed and she looked down the length of him then back at his unconscious face.

He looked younger and curiously defenceless and she felt a flood of tenderness for him that she'd never known before, because he'd gone through the darkness of a bad marriage and fought the demons it had left him with to come through—for her.

Then his eyes opened and he lifted his head and looked around dazedly until his gaze fell on her. And an expression of sheer relief flooded his smoky grey eyes. 'Clare? Are you OK?'

'I'm fine and I love you quite desperately,' she said softly.

'I love you the same way. I—'

But a nurse bustled in with two very upset bundles which she put into the cot. 'OK, folks,' she said. 'We're going to freshen you up, Mrs Hewitt, and check you out, then the fun really begins! Our first feed. I tell you what, they may be small but they're like little tigers this morning. Now, I know your milk hasn't come in yet but...'

As she went on to explain about the mysteries of breast-feeding, Clare and Lachlan looked at each other wryly, then smiled and held hands.

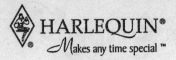 **HARLEQUIN®**
Makes any time special ™

In celebration of Harlequin®'s golden anniversary

Enter to win a *dream!* You could win:

- A luxurious trip for two to
  The Renaissance Cottonwoods Resort
  in Scottsdale, Arizona, or

- A bouquet of flowers once a week for a year
  from **FTD**, or

- A $500 shopping spree, or

- A fabulous bath & body gift basket, including
  K-tel's *Candlelight and Romance* 5-CD set.

Look for **WIN A DREAM** flash on
specially marked Harlequin® titles by
Penny Jordan, Dallas Schulze,
Anne Stuart and Kristine Rolofson
in October 1999*.

FTD **RENAISSANCE.**
COTTONWOODS RESORT **K·TEL**
SCOTTSDALE, ARIZONA

*No purchase necessary—for contest details send a self-addressed envelope to
Harlequin Makes Any Time Special Contest, P.O. Box 9069, Buffalo, NY, 14269-9069
(include contest name on self-addressed envelope). Contest ends December 31, 1999.
Open to U.S. and Canadian residents who are 18 or over. Void where prohibited.

PHMATS-GR

HARLEQUIN PRESENTS®

Seduction
SWEET ~~REVENGE~~

They wanted to get even.
Instead they got...married!

by bestselling author

Penny Jordan

Don't miss Penny Jordan's latest enthralling miniseries
about four special women. Kelly, Anna, Beth and Dee
share a bond of friendship and a burning desire to
avenge a wrong. But in their quest for revenge, they
each discover an even stronger emotion.
Love.

Look out for all four books in Harlequin Presents®:

November 1999
THE MISTRESS ASSIGNMENT

December 1999
LOVER BY DECEPTION

January 2000
A TREACHEROUS SEDUCTION

February 2000
THE MARRIAGE RESOLUTION

Available at your favorite retail outlet.

HARLEQUIN®
Makes any time special ™

Coming Next Month

HARLEQUIN PRESENTS®

THE BEST HAS JUST GOTTEN BETTER!

**#2061 THE MISTRESS ASSIGNMENT Penny Jordan
(Sweet Revenge/Seduction)**
Kelly has agreed to act the seductress in order to teach a
lesson to the man who betrayed her best friend. It's a scheme
fraught with danger—especially when gorgeous stranger
Brough Frobisher gets caught in the cross fire....

**#2062 THE REVENGE AFFAIR Susan Napier
(Presents Passion)**
Joshua Wade was convinced that Regan was plotting to disrupt
their wedding. Regan had to admit there was unfinished
business between them—a reckless one-night stand.... She had
good reason for getting close to Joshua, though, but she could
never reveal her secret plans....

**#2063 SLADE BARON'S BRIDE Sandra Marton
(The Barons)**
When Lara Stevens and Slade Baron were both facing an
overnight delay in an airport, Slade suggested they spend the
time together. Who would she hurt if Lara accepted his
invitation? He wanted her, and she wanted . . . his child!

**#2064 THE BOSS'S BABY Miranda Lee
(Expecting!)**
When Olivia's fiancé ditched her, her world had been blown
apart and with it, her natural caution. She'd gone to the office
party and seduced her handsome boss! But now Olivia has a
secret she dare not tell him!

#2065 THE SECRET DAUGHTER Catherine Spencer
Soon after Joe Donnelly's sizzling night with Imogen Palmer,
she'd fled. Now ten years on, Joe was about to uncover an
astonishing story—one that would culminate in a heartrending
reunion with the daughter he never knew he had.

**#2066 THE SOCIETY GROOM Mary Lyons
(Society Weddings)**
When Olivia meets her former lover, rich socialite Dominic
FitzCharles, at a society wedding, he has a surprise for her: he
announces their betrothal to the press, in front of London's
elite. Just how is Olivia supposed to say no?